Kotch
The Imagery of Trouble

by

Richard Page

DORRANCE PUBLISHING CO., INC.
PITTSBURGH, PENNSYLVANIA 15222

ISBN: 978-1-4349-0822-3
eISBN: 978-1-4349-5576-0
Printed in the United States of America

First Printing

For more information or to order additional books, please contact:
Dorrance Publishing Co., Inc.
701 Smithfield Street
Pittsburgh, Pennsylvania 15222
U.S.A.
1-800-788-7654
www.dorrancebookstore.com

To my wife, family, and friends.

Synopsis

A new prototype of passenger aircraft has been developing secretly. This aircraft uses major nuclear propulsion as fuel for the twenty-first century and beyond. The aircraft, though, would carry uncommon security hazard and risk spreading its technology and getting into the hands of Al-Qaeda, which would not only lay bare as a threat to the west and the rest of the known world.

The entire big operator agreed that while the concept is honourable because of security risk, it would investigate the feasible aspects and see if the threat could be lessened in view of the ratio of the probability found during the investigation.

Brandon Willows and his wife, Shank, who is an illegitimate daughter of policeman Borer Hamilton, are given the job. They usually work for the environmental ministry, mainly on discovering particulates dumped in the waterways and in other restricted areas by unscrupulous dealers. However, they have left that employment and set up their own detective agency called WPIA. They are friends of Borer, too, who operates another secret security agency in the surveillance industry.

There is suspicion that a cartel is set up somewhere that proposes to get the prototype aircraft's secrets and sell them to Al-Qaeda. Though not proven, Borer is given the task to help in the search. Fritz who is Brandon's cousin wears many faces of deception, with covert manipulation and deeds of devious elements behind him. However, he knows his way around and he could become useful to the cause, even though Brandon's trust in him remains nil.

Brandon and Shank are reluctant to take on the big job, but Borer wheeled in with a big stick and got them to take on the job, with him being the driver. Almost overnight, they were caught up in a rampant imagery of trouble; meantime Shank becomes pregnant with a pregnancy that seems bent on causing trouble, but before all that, she was working almost twenty-four hours each day with Brandon to help him sort out the problem since she expects the worst of her life's problems.

Prologue

ORIGIN

Hi, Kotch. What is your storyline this time? I know...I know writers write what others fear to say.

KOTCH

It is about a guy called Brandon and his wife, a police sergeant's illegitimate daughter, Shank. This story is set in an English city outskirt. They set up a little detective agency to flush out a person who drops off rubbish and dumps particulates in waterways and rivers. Their intention seems ominous and straightforward enough until his father-in-law, a policeman, twisted their arms, forcing them to take on a big investigative job. Trouble is never far away from them, but let them tell you its origin.

It was an exciting afternoon. Brandon was on his way to the fish and chip shop. The day was as normal and good as the autumn leaves falling to the ground. The yellow leaves were as happy; as I was going along, I noticed them dancing as they leave the branches and fell to the ground when I came out through our front door. The sun was shining blissfully and humbly across the valley and to the distant hills; far into the distances into the shadow of the scenery, all the trees were shedding their yellow leaves to the earth. Funny how one might have taken these things for granted as I used to do, and when one then banged up away for a few weeks, then it is like a resurrected mind that viewed and appreciated every little thing the eyes saw, then beholding the leaves leaving its mother branches.

Chapter One

"My name's Brandon, and my wife's Shank. We are from Willows Private Investigation Agency (WPIA). We worked under the banned substances squad, part of an investigating program that apprehended those who dumped particulate waste in rivers and other waterways and places illegally. Sometimes, we got onto the drug-crime raid in the suburban districts and elsewhere. It was an inner city incumbency.

"My first real job came when Shank, my wife, asked me to get a bit of lunch from one of our local chip shop. She was running things when I was away, and now she was behaving as though she was the boss. Nonetheless, she loves me so much. Since I came home, I wasn't quite sure how to handle the immediate future anymore. It seemed simply doing a turn for my wife. What could be simpler than that? And it was for a woman who covered me with so much love that she was becoming unkind.

"She was all over me since I got out of the soaped-up charge the police had on me and was bricked up for a couple of weeks behind one of Her majesty's pen. I took the rap for a local friend who would see me right after I got out, but because my reputation was almost perfect, I got off lightly and without any future repercussion to follow up streams. That friend got so many pending charges against himself that even after Judgement Day, he might be the only criminal left in prison, or in the world, and he knew it; he wouldn't die because of those charges if the authorities got hold of him, and if they did not, then he was sure to live for eternity to serve his time. But that was then, and I got out without any broken limbs, without continuing to look to see who or what was following behind.

"Mussolini ran the Good Fries shop ten minutes away and back on foot. But there was not ten minutes to spare for me, for I got people to see and catch up with and five minutes away from Shank was a bit draining. Say about half that in Shank's car, a new vehicle she had picked up a couple of days before I came out. I couldn't wait to get behind the wheel and drive that luxurious-looking model. It was still gleaming from the shines, with its deep blue finishing, and the smell of the inner décor was quite aromatic; I wanted to get my arse in on the new leathers and, with authority, to drive. I longed to see Mussolini and get some run down from outside Shank's details and that of others who have tried to feed me on their visits, as well as to do a bit of show-offs in our brand new spanking vehicle.

"Fish with chips are what we Brits eat as a quick fix meal, possibly with a couple cans of soda, mainly from the Pepsi or cola assortments. Otherwise, my meal is also known in English as French fries just across the port of Dover, potato cut up in small squares bits and then fried. Never bothered to find out why the heck they called it French fries and why they did not call it American fry-ups since it was discovered there and brought back to Europe by Walter Raleigh, Marco Polo, Francis Drake or some other damn adventurer. Shank woke up that morning and yawned haughtily, saying she was feeling good.

"Well, I didn't like to hear a woman talking about 'feeling good.' All blokes knew that when his woman's saying that, within the day, all hell would break loose and third world war could come at any time, without preparation to defend themselves in running the day-to-day chores. Then they had given no time to set up any missile silos and other war tools, as that of the frying pans, and no bunker for the generals to hide themselves from the female missiles: no defence for a bloke.

"Shank was determined to finish off our first assignment—the counting up of the work she have done for the PD. She was now working on the topping up of the bills to send off our first invoice to the squad. Albeit, it had just gone into a warm autumn's midday sunshine when I pulled the vehicle off the drive, not knowing what would happen at the end of the day. At the time, whether Shank and I would be so palled before the day closed was hovering in my mind. Anyway, I dismissed it. But then, I commenced to view it as an ideal, yet regrettable feeling as soon as it entered my mind since she was much more kind and responsive than ever from our previous encounters. We were too solid in love and friendship— just what a bloke needed when he came home to his miss to break away from remembering the prison episode.

"There was nothing else on the road more than the Almighty, gravity, sunshine, myself, and a calm wind whistling, stirring and shaking the trees that were shedding their yellow autumn leaves in the main. It was approximately five minutes when I noticed that a battered old Ford saloon was following closely behind. It carried no front bumper, and as far as I could quickly observe, the occupants could be seen standing up over the dashboard. Its gurgle and spluttering crossed the calm engineered sounds of our new vehicle that was almost silently running. When I had stopped at the traffic light, it was showing amber. Then it dropped into red. Normal.

"The view of the chip shop came on the opposite corner where I passed and sometimes waved to the billionaire who hadn't got a penny to his name, or so he told us anyway. I could see Mussolini's employees working away, dipping in and out of the showcase as customers stretched almost to the outside doorway in the queues. Paying less concern to what it was that would be coming along to disturb the tranquil noonday, and from that time on, the imagery of trouble was not too far behind.

"An old Cortina distributes polluting smoke as fire in a forest. The low wind took the blue smoke and whiffed it in front of the saloon. Then, a little part particle drove and just passed in and caught my nostril. Scientists called it 'parts per billion,' but I reckoned it must be 'parts per ten.' Balls of the stuff were floating and coming forward faster than I could outrun it. It went up and followed up by showering more granules, shadowing over Shank's motor just as the vehicle I was in stopped, getting ready for the next change of the stoplights to green.

"'My turn...come on...come on,' I said. I was thinking I was encouraging the lights to turn onto green, but as fate would have it, I was encouraging the battered Ford to get closer and closer and closer to me."

Chapter Two

BRANDON

Oh shit! I know it! I know it! Not in Shank's motor!

."I surmised that the Ford wasn't going to stop unless something was there to stop it, and with equal impact, it was trying to space out the vehicle behind. It was no calmer than to realize that's Shank's brand new vehicle with me inside the darn metal box stood in its path and the lights seemingly stuck and parked itself on the red. Shank restricted me from swearing, becoming what she came to call me as 'foul mouthed Brandon.' But what I picked up when around other inmates would take weeks to clear, as well as get back to my old lungs and normalise myself again, a sort of demobbing."

SHANK

You look just like 'em. You talk like 'em. You eat like 'em. You even walk like 'em.

BRANDON

Do I make love like 'em?

SHANK

I don't know about that. Never made love to any prisoner before.

BRANDON

Oh, my gaud, it's coming for me!

"It was then I quickly pulled the handbrake and prepared for the impact. It has ended with a great banging crash and the Almighty juddered, with a silence that only a dead person would understand. I felt myself; I was alive. Then I began to blow lots of dragons after. I knew of a sort that I was not dead. My blood entered the veins and curdles, then stiffened the respiratory system like a good piece of steel bar held out by a trembling hand."

BRANDON

Can I see your driving document, buster? And please, don't say anything right now beside what is compulsory. Your documents?

"I said to myself what I would say. I kicked the door open of the car and then I walked from the front, just in case it was a really madman after me. I suspected if he was, he would run me down should he have gotten no insurance. Nowadays, people would refer to it as 'road rage' at a civil level."

BRANDON

Are you nuts? Are...you blind? Can't you see?

"I forgot what I was going to say, but then I spat it out in a stammering tongue of a fashion. He must have understood; he was dreading up. Being of the same creed, I had to cool down fast. My blood was circulating as if it was frictional, getting hot, and it was taking everything up to the heart. There and then, a small carcass appeared out of the bent-up saloon and rust bucket."

MAN (*in Jamaican accent*)

Me? Name is Steve Boot, Mr. Willows.

"He came around to the half side and stretched his hand out for me to grab it. Normally, I would've grabbed it, but I kept it back for defence. He was speaking in lingual patois, a Jamaican dialect which I know very well. Shank, my wife, could not have understood much of the wording used; she was born in England and never yet travelled the western Caribbean's to learn the real patois."

STEVE

I kind of....No, have none a them tings, you know, Sur. Me a trying fe gets your attention from you, pull off the drive, but me hon' is not working. Su I decided to ram you down.

BRANDON

Could've killed me in the process, Steve! I can't see why you got no insurance. Got no breaking device, not even compression with that damn car. Oh, Steve, that's the end of me!

STEVE

Me hears say you are a good man, you know. And I got a little job for you. Don't worry about that little problem—bout the motor. It will get fixe.

But fey me, the problem is big things. And you half tries and help me to get out of it, you know, so...

BRANDON

Oh, oh! Hold on! You're asking me to do a job for you, yeah? And you smashed my wife's motor up, yeah? And you just said to me not to worry? Yes? You know my wife? No? You know that she's going to eat me first and have you for supper or dessert, do away with both of us? Who's wrong—that isn't the matter.

"I wobbled my index finger at face level."

BRANDON

All I know is we are going to be eaten alive. Got it? It is a death cert. Did you say you got a job? Let's talk.

STEVE

It's a small thing that you will work out with your woman. You and your miss, man. But see it, yaw? Right now, things has gone badly for me. I just come out a prison and I caught the woman with him. This man was in my bed. So I just anointed both a them with my weapon I did have in de garage.

BRANDON

You didn't kill them now, did you, Steve?

STEVE

Me nu knows if the man is dead or mashed up because he jumped out of de windows, when me a flagged de woman. Way, I want you to do is to find out who the man is and whom he connected to. If he is alive, he's very lucky. But a look, yeah, he must be in de hospital. So fine him a for me, nu?

"While Steve and myself were conversing, we managed to push the old Ford off the main road into an alleyway. Then I managed to convince Steve that he should return with me to the office; it was to get Shank and tell her that I had nothing to do with the motor damage. Shank saw her car when we got back and did not recognize it had been changed to an unbelievable wreck. She peered through the office's window. The rear end of the vehicle was widening out as if it had been hit by a low loader. I explained later at the office."

BRANDON

Look, babe, I didn't hurt your motor. It is this man—a new client and customer. You can eat him before you kill him. But spare me the chance to explain before the main course, sweetheart!

SHANK
    What is this wreck? This is not my brand new car! No, no, no! It can't be!

"She fluffed and went Sputniks. Then she started to speak something sounding like Russian. I don't speak the language, so I didn't understand. But I guessed she might be saying something about her motor being smashed and I was responsible."

BRANDON
    Well, it was like this…

"I started to explain."

BRANDON
    Then that it was like that.

Chapter Three

SHANK

I'm not having any of that from none a 'yaw. All I want, by 'morrow, I want to see my motor fix. Got it? I got to get to Wales next day after 'morrow; I want to use it. You better fix it by then. Look at it!

"She was in her raging bad moments, and for a while, I kept calm, allowing her to breathe out the rage I thought she might be accumulating somehow."

BRANDON

See what you have done?

"I turned to and asked Steve; he looked at me and might have seen the dying look on my face."

STEVE

I'll raise the money, sis. But, it can't fix now until this. Man here takes the job me a give him to do. In de morning, I will bring him about ten grand as a deposit. Laud woman, Oona, cries cries too much, fey little things like this. De ca-car is noting big. Char!

SHANK

And could I ask you, Sir Steve, where you're going to get ten thousand pounds as deposit? You're driving an old wreck, slammed into my motor with no licence, no insurance. This is serious shit!

STEVE

Hold on, sis. Who tells you I don't have any licence, and I don't have any bread?

"He pulled a wallet from the inside of his overcoat pocket, took out his license, and showed it."

STEVE

Then what is this, big sister? This is a legitimate document, isn't it? Why you woman always a bawl? A bawl, so.... This not no big, big things.

"I wanted Shank to go easy; it was my first big break on my own bat. I then threw a whisper to her ear. I was immediately drawn to Steve for being truthful and would like to have given him the benefit of the doubt."

BRANDON

Turn it down a bit, honey.

"I told her, but she didn't. So I ordered her when her temper flew vertical and horizontal before completely going off the scale of elevation. It was then that I walked away and had lunch for my dinner. Six days after being in the shithouse building bunkers, except the day when I didn't have any material. That was it. When Steve came, the day had been blown into calamity surgery. However, the following morning, Steve came early to see me; I was still earning my keeps. For the first time outside accountancy, I've never seen such wads of fifties and twenties in raw cash at one time."

BRANDON

Did you pull a job, Steve?

STEVE

Whey 'you a talk 'bout, Mr. Willows?

"He asked me, behaving as if that question should not even be mentioned, much less be asked."

BRANDON

Steve. I wonder... Grab a seat.

STEVE

Whey'ono. Always a wonder, wonder whey this come from and whey that come from. If me just come out a prison, whey me a fey has time to pull any things this big? Den n'ono can check it out, if it is genuine or legit. Whey me wants you fey does is to find the man who I knocked my miss off. I believe is a friend's father. Me not going to kill him but me going to write me friends and tell them what a take place out 'yaw.

BRANDON

You want us to review your case and find a man? How long you've been away?

STEVE

It is six years I get, but due to behaving myself, I only spend nearly half of dot. Me never guilty. But them says I did, and the boys in blue beat me up when them arrest me. Is not dot only. I believe dot the woman a work some guzzo on me, too.

"Shank was doing background listening in the next apartment—her own office. It was then when she got up and stood at the door, holding on to the swinging, half-open door while Steve and I conversed. I was still digging a little bit deeper to find out whether I should take the job on or not. At that point, I was in a position to either refuse or accept with open arms Steve's dilemmas straight away. We were warned not to touch any judiciary matters; Borer, our policeman friend and Shank's unknown father, had thrown in that piece without charge before us set up the operation."

BORER

Too involved, Willows. Take up too much good time and paper throwing. A cop who worth his salt will know it; he's avoiding the judiciary matter like a plague. But he got to work with it. You, though, don't have to be in court every day.

"I was in a dilemma, too. Shank would be riding the train to Wales the next day. She decided that after the mishap, she wasn't going to drive any beaten-up motors to meet her client for the first time. We were partners in the business; we would be working as such, but it was between Shank and me. The motor was with Steve and me to fix for Shank's cooperation, with a whole lot of lollies lying in front of me; more was promised. Steve believed that his woman was doing something paranormal to him. However, he could not identify what it was that she's supposed to have been doing."

SHANK

Did you mention that she might be working something on you?

STEVE

Dot is exactly what me a say. De woman—look, even in a prison—dot black crows cum a taunt me when I go outside.

"It was then that something had turned to the unusual and got me beaten. For a little while, a crow came on the roof of the next-door building, crowing and cooing like a young baby."

STEVE

See it, d'ye? Dot's it. The same one. Anywhere I go, it cum balling at me. And I believe dot de woman doing it to get her hands on me money.

BRANDON

Steve? You must not let your imagination runs riot within you.

SHANK

What we are talking about? Like how much money's involved?

STEVE

I can't tell you dot. Dot a fey me private concern. Su whoa happens? You're goin' take the job on? I would be glad if you take it on, for me hears that you were down in the West Indies. You must sort 'a know something about how dem work de guzzo to investigate dis. One way me a talk 'bout.

BRANDON

Steve, we weren't set up to deal with this sort of investigation—paranormal glitches. It's outside our limit. If that's the case, see a vicar or a parson. We'll do some prod for you and will come back if we can find the man you've beaten up. All you do is to get Shank's motor fixed and get yourself some organizing. We have to discuss it as you're a man of means. Leave it a while with us.

STEVE

If you nu quickly wid it, me a go fine me self-back in the de prison before you get to what I am saying to you. Treat it as urgent, man.

SHANK

We'll do what we can. How can we find you or get more information, Steve?

STEVE

I jack up with a friend from last night. I will get in touch. Believe the boys in blue must be searching for me if he did die, but is not me would 'a kill him.

"Instead of using our energy on the mundane motor repair, we must now turn our attention to helping with Steve's dilemmas. Ten grand in bundles was lying on the table for the taking. Shank was easier to deal with from then on—absolutely so. Shank would be leaving early the next morning on the train bound for Wales following some consideration the evening before. Steve left another three thousand for the car's fixing and for the job to be done quickly. Money wasn't the objective any longer at this instance; the car was. It was evening."

Chapter Four

STEVE

You can get things in England if you got money. Pay de man a little bit more and get your wife case sort out quickly. As you can see, is not de money I don't have. But if I spend it and buy a new motor, who is going to drive it when I'm back in prison? Nobody! De woman can't drive; only me the sister a drive round de bend. I can't spend the money when I'm in prison, so I'm giving you dot privilege to spend what you can to set me free.

"Steve was obviously petrified. When Steve supplied us with the information, continuously, I keyed in some telephone numbers and started to dial those I found from the local directory on my desk."

BRANDON

Ha! It's Willows here. Trying to find from the emergency side someone who may come in from the Minsworth area about two nights ago. A man, a black man. Pick up anybody from that area about that time. Anything of that nature?

VOICE FROM HOSPITAL

Relatives? Got to look it up for you, Sir.

BRANDON

Just a friend. Got anything?

HOSPITAL

A Caucasian was picked up around the time you identify. Nothing came in from that area since.

BRANDON
No, it's a black man, I think, I'm sure I want to hear about.

"I then spurred my viewpoint, whether I'd been given the correct information or not."

HOSPITAL
After treatment for a broken ankle, he discharged himself, though. Very strange man, strange indeed—Mr. Massey; he was very badly beaten. Had a broken ankle. Still, he managed to get the doctors to discharge him.

BRANDON
Naw, that's not him. Not him at all.

"I then spent the rest of the day searching for Steve to find out the nationality or creed of the person we were talking about. Since we were assuming he was from an ethnic culture and since I read somewhere that a Pope has declared that all things outside Europe belong to Europe, whether it was inside or outside of the continent, it was evidently a European, we concluded."

Later that evening...

STEVE
Yes, it is a white man, Su. But him son is my friend. In the prison, me meet him. It makes me turn on the woman.

BRANDON
How long this is going on?

STEVE
Since me wins de little money, she takes him on. Muss a fey kill me so that dem can enjoy demself. Every minute, me a see de black bird cum a bawl, bawl. But they're not getting any of de money. Dem not getting one penny to spend and have dem sweet time while me is un-free.

"I telephoned another hospital in the local area to pursue the investigation. Remembering the receptionist, I browsed over the name of Mr. Massey. It allowed me to ask directly, having a name in mind and sources from the onset."

STEVE
If is my friend father, den yes. Him name is Massey. Tony Massey. But him a big man, you know. Him is one of dem big and high up in de law things. But him son not no paying him any mind. A real rough neck, but I and him get on good. He let me know a few scores in the law tings. Si

whey me a say, you'll be up against some big people who want me out a de way. John crow Nam dem supper.

"Shank's own investigation was cooled down. Shank's client in Wales put off her divorce on the cool for a month. By then, she would give Shank more information about where her husband was dumping his assets abroad. It allowed her time to join me while still getting payment from her client's continuous engagement."

SHANK
Steve has reminded me of Jupt. Can't get closer?

BRANDON
Some of us have the same media training. If you were educated at Oxford, then you would be and behave like an Oxfordian, and so would your colleagues and friends. I call that tribalism, which is still inherently so in some. H.M.P.S.-trained (Her Majesty's Prison Service).

SHANK
I guess you're right. What did Steve do to go to prison?

"She twitched her shoulder and stared at me, something she did when she got a point to clear hollowly."

SHANK
Did he beat up his old lady?

BRANDON
You mean his wife? Ask him when you see him again. He might tell you. As our slates weren't so clean, I couldn't do that.

SHANK
What do you mean? We've served our time, and boy, it's time for us to put it under the bridge!

BRANDON
Glad to do that, but it seems we are going to deal with all sorts of these types. I was part educated there as well; don't forget that. I can understand the vocabulary, the lingo, and the frustration; speak the language, doll.

SHANK
Your choice got no excuse for not making a buck out of it. There is plenty of this game about: prisoner versus the establishment.

"Meanwhile, a car pulled up outside our office park. It was evening."

SHANK
What he wants now?

"She was asking maliciously. It was Borer."

SHANK
I thought it was the last we've seen of him. Think he was going to butt out and leave us alone with things or give us a breather. Now, here, the louse showed up in the head.

BRANDON
Babe, cool it a bit; he's our guiding angel...until we manage to stand on our four feet, doll. Until we can stand on our two feet, that's all.

"Borer, she knew, spelled 'trouble' in a big way. She walked to the door and opened it."

BORER
Got anything on at the moment?

"He was standing and leant slightly, resting his close fist onto the door facing us."

SHANK
Depend. Scotch or tea—which, Sir?

BORER
A tipple on the rock. But would you like to take on something big? I mean big in income, class, and get to meet some people? I want you to know them—up the ladder and in the know. It will keep you out of the court-house, with a good income as well.

SHANK
Might consider.

BRANDON
Hold on a minute. Heard of blokes giving little outfits like us a big break only for them to end on the rail. We want to take our time, got it? Lots of lose about, DIB. One swallow and they gulp you down in one mouthful.

"Then, Borer hinted that he would be retiring soon. How soon? We were uncertain when it would be. He was our shot to the star—to please or not to please. The policeman sat remaining alert when Shank tipped the whisky bottle and handed it over."

BORER

Keep out a this one, Brandon Willows. It's a break you must consider Shank. Don't want you blaming me for your returning to your old ways and drag this poor sweet girl down there with you again. Obviously, I'd prefer her to decide rather than you, Willows.

BRANDON

Gaud dam it. Burning the bad lamp for me, aren't you? When you blokes going to let go, DIB?

BORER

When you come up with this one, chum. Set you up for life. Then I can say I'd done my bit; I helped a Black man for the rest of his life.

"He handed a piece of paper in codifying intelligence to Shank."

BORER

Drugs need vehicle, trains, boat ships, aircraft, and men to operate it across the globe. You name it, and they'll want some sort of transport to do it with.

Chapter Five

SHANK

Can see that? But Blacks don't have none a them. Yet they've filled the prison up and down the country. If the drug baron has all these, they must be supplying the Blacks.

BRANDON

Lots. Some dead men, too.

BORER

How's your chap down that side? Heard from Qualm? She's taking him on. I mean, marrying him, next month, I think it'll be. Going?

"He was referring to Jupt and Auntie Guam's story which developed during the back and forth, coming and going from the Caribbean."

SHANK

Home office still holding onto our passport, Sir. They indicated that we may have to ask someone to help sort it out for us.

BORER

Take this piece on, and I'll talk to my boss to see if we can arrange a temporary one. See how you get on. Gaud, man, doesn't look as you're dead.

"I took the couple of A4 sheets instruction he'd handed to Shank."

BRANDON

Never! This will take years!

BORER

That's what you want, don't you? To get your feet under the table? Don't let it frighten you. He who walks a thousand miles got to make the first step. Never can quite remember where that saying came, but it's good for any job.

BRANDON

Sure, but not this big. If we fail...

BORER

Did I hear you say fail? The lazy man said, "Looks like there is a lion out in the square, and I won't go out today." Think you will say the same, Brandon Willows?

BRANDON

That's what...

SHANK

We must thank you for considering giving us this big chance. But you see, if we fail...

BORER

Don't worry about failure; BAID (British and American Intelligent Data) will fund any incurred expenditure.

"He tapped his fingers on the table a few times, as though he was playing the piano keyboard."

BORER

Turning your little outfit into a megabuck investigation agency for industrial espionage game. Think you'll manage? Use your experience in camouflage. Of course, you're a man of experience, Willows, master of disguised heart.

BRANDON

The drug industry's big enough for us to cope, DIB. Especially, Shank's going down the matrimonial route, you know? Just signed up a big contract. Didn't you, doll? And I've just taken on a really hot potato earlier. Can't drop them like that; know what I mean, DIB?

BORER

You two could send a man to drink, smoke to his early grave, or do something else.

SHANK

I'm just scared of taking on. At this early stage...such large, swelling up expenses, Sir.

BORER

Ever consider I have confidence that you will be able to carry out this assignment?

"I looked over at Shank who's still holding the glass with Borer's second drink. He knew we have transmitted unseen information above his head. He stretched his hand out and almost broke her fingers apart from the glass."

BORER

There are many fishes in the sea, you two. Many sharks, too.

BRANDON

Not anymore. Not as much as it used to be. Men take them out one after the other with their harpoons nowadays.

BORER

What's wrong with you two? Gone holy on me again? While I'm around, things will be all right; I'll see to that.

SHANK

No, Sir. We're just being cautious.

BRANDON

Yeah, just being cautious. Nothing wrong with that, is there?

BORER

Too damn cautious, I must say.

SHANK

And we're prudent, as well.

"She smiled. Borer caught her following a simple sip he took from the glass. He then knew that we would be considering his proposal by our shared communication style. He left us to consider his offer, of us going to BAID."

BORER

You must consider. Need a reply by noon tomorrow.

"He got up from the chair. Meanwhile, we considered Steve's case and his reliance on us to sort thing out. Then it was evening."

SHANK
Start off with being an honest broker?

"I looked at her admiringly. Steve showed up just as Borer left. The telephone rang a couple of times; Shank took it."

SHANK
There's somebody for you.

BRANDON
Who is it?

SHANK
Don't know; didn't ask. Sound as if he knows you.

BRANDON
Can I help?

FRITZ
Fritz here, my man. Good to hear that you're back and holding your own. How's things going, old man?

BRANDON
Well, I am stunned. Blow my dirty sock. Glad to know that you're still around, Fritz. Leave the green since you help to send me down. Spend my two extra years in there, mate. Weren't looking for you to call me, and don't bother with the family stuff. Nah. Not going to work this time.

FRITZ
Know what they say? A bad coin always turns up somewhere. How's the outfit going? With all that money you're earning now, should be pretty good sailing on here in.

BRANDON
I thought they hanged you long time ago and your bones were crushed with some motor part, lying in ash, wrought iron tray or somewhere else as somebody's table legs, you dirty, immoral chameleon. You dirty rag.

"Fritz laughed loudly; Shank cringed."

BRANDON
I can't handle you just yet. I got responsibilities now, cousin.

FRITZ
Never know you were the marrying type, Bran.

SHANK

Who's he.... That's the one you were asking about from Borer? Does Borer know? I guess he does, doesn't he?

BRANDON

Yeah, that's him. The bastard.

STEVE

The big fish gets cleaned and the little fish gets fed—mutual benefit. But the big one will Nam you, too.

"He mumbled out just before he left. After the encounter with Fritz, Steve declared that he would be coming back early the next day. Then, evening came.

"He went by, climbed over the fencing at the rear of the building, and then disappeared. It was at home that evening when Shank and I got our first big blowout since the motor vehicle crisis. Fritz called, saying we were causing big problems. It was hard to explain, and I didn't try understanding it, either. Couldn't win? The past was rolling and rolling and fast to catch up with Fritz's story. He was the sort of hoodlum one would like to restore and at the same time would like to destroy, but it was like dead shit in the pants."

SHANK

You've got to get rid of him—him or me. Did you ring him up? I mean Fritz, Brandon Willows. Tell me a lie, and I swear I'll get rid of you.

BRANDON

Hold on, sweetheart. Didn't even know whether the guy's dead or alive. Ever heard of a prisoner dilemma, doll? Could be dead voice there for all intent and purpose.

SHANK

Sucked hell from you and your mates. Not anymore. I've got lots of the dilemmas, too, you know?

BRANDON

Sorry, babe. Won't happen again.

"I put my hands out and held hers; she responded. I knew, though, that her threats would remain a problem for the future."

BRANDON

How about this big assignment? We've to talk about it. Borer wants an answer 'morrow.

SHANK

Need a break? We need a few good cases under our belt for reference. BAID could give us that ripple. Those are big guys. Can't mess with them though; mess them up and you won't eat food again and end up in concrete blocks holding up some motorways.

Chapter Six

"It was midnight when we decided to take on the big fish. The BAID assignment, we assumed Borer believed we weren't going to take on. We discussed how he might shit in his pants when we told him so. The evening closed the day with a few glasses of sherry from the cheaper assortments which I picked up from our local superstore."

BRANDON
You're not going to blame me for that, would you now?"

SHANK
I'll blame you if you delay coming to bed two minutes from now. Professors.... What did you say, Bran?

BRANDON
Fritz looked surprised; that's good. Believe someone higher up in BAID.

SHANK
I said provisos, not professors.

"With contempt, Shank and I went to meet Fritz a few days after he made his first contact with us. He took Shank's hands as if he had known her for a long time, and that made me feel uncomfortable from the top of my head to the soles of my feet."

FRITZ
Something like that rings a bell in my ears. I've been looking for that clause a long time.

"Fritz's hand eased away from Shank's shoulder. He walked towards me; my guard was fully up. He turned and opened the door leading to the bar."

FRITZ

Anyone can make mistakes, Bran.

BRANDON

Yeah, but not with your blood relations. Not in my book, you crooked son of a bitch.

FRITZ

That maybe my mum you're talking about, old boy. You're the nephew; son of that bitch is your aunt, which makes us first cousins. But we have the same—a bad one: bad blood. Been from my dad's side; I could disown him for that.

SHANK

Come on now, guys. You two got to look forward the blazing the trail together. Done it before; can be done again.

BRANDON

She's joking, I believe. Got it? Not in a million years.

FRITZ

I'll buy the pub lunch today if you promised not to get lunch out of arguing.

SHANK

You're not going to treat him to a free lunch? Thought I was worth more than.... Shut up or....

"Shank's mobile started to spit decibels."

BRANDON

Shank. Hey, inspector? Yes, he's with us. Want him? Fritz, for you. Borer wants you.

FRITZ

Yes, inspector? Trying to bring him round to our way of thinking. When she's coming in? Let me talk to him. Yeah. I'll have to do some negotiating.

"He smiled, his feature changing from placid to sombre then back to normal. She walked up to the counter and ordered pouched eggs, bacon, toast, and beans. I couldn't believe how fast I'd gulped the food to get Shank away from her newfound friend, Fritz, and back to reality."

Later, at the police station…

"Fritz caught the train home. Shank waved him off, but I didn't. Shank and I then tried to abandon the day. However, when we got home later, the answering machine was quite busy. Steve had been caught and locked up in jail for attempted murder of Rene Massy. He wanted me to be his legal guardian, but it was deep water for us and we had no intention of considering the case any further. Nonetheless, I had a rethink."

Later…

"When I reached the police station, Shank was arrested as an accomplice; she was shielding Steve. I could not get bail for her, and she had to wait to be given bail by the magistrate court the next day; that's what I was told by the jail keeper."

SHANK

> I think our world's collapsing on us, around us! We're on the centre of the cosmos. Borer's getting his way here. Damn it, Dad! I can smell his hands full with our downfall. Make no mistake; he has got something to do with this one. Definitely! I think Steve was a plant from Borer and company.

BRANDON

> Leopards can't change their spot, doll. Reckon he's going to get to us sooner or later if we don't comply—bent cops.

SHANK

> Never bent yourself; you would defend him for your right. Depend on which foot is wearing the boot to kick one up the bum.

"Fritz got on the telephone with Borer earlier on. Just as the train settled down on its journey with him going home, his mobile vibrated. They were talking about us, thinking how to create more problems so we would exclude any other who wanted our service, including Steve."

BORER

> Take Brandon out first; believe me, the woman will bow.

FRITZ

> Think she will?

BORER

> Positive.

Fritz

> I'd say take the chic out first. Think he loves the woman more than she loves him; sensed that right away. He'll come round to our way of building the team.

"Meanwhile, I left Shank at the police station and went off to find Fritz. I caught the late train to Charlton but did not request any assistance or any of Borer's benevolent help.

"I was thinking about Shank, concerned, and even though Fritz was as an enemy, we were still related in the flesh. Grudges and malice could only go so far; somebody at sometime had to give in or commit to the inevitable.

"At the early hours of the morning, we went to the address Fritz had given to Shank. It was aside an old industrial estate, the taxi driver revealed. Some parts were in use, but a large acreage had been empty for some time. The vehicle turned off the main road onto the old rundown estate road."

Later that evening...

Taxi Driver

> Believe me, Gov. Nothing is down this place beside ghost and darkness. Never saw anybody coming nor going. It's a world out there of its own. Only boys play down here at night. Sort of funny area to be visiting at this hour.

Chapter Seven

"Fritz knew all about us as though he'd set out as to spy; we guessed Borer was behind it all. When Shank pulled onto the public house's car park, we saw a slim, bearded man walking toward our vehicle. He was tall and got the looks of a cricketer. His father has gone and farting on his mother, running off with a seventeen years old kitchen hand girl.

"My aunt, I know, was devastated of the events that followed. Fritz was as a screwed-up kid as his old man. He was bent on taking revenge on both sides of his family. It had seemed to be the only pick he had."

Brandon recalls what Aunt Maud said…

AUNT MAUD
> He had a turbulent time growing up, Brandon. You have to forgive him for what he had done. This beastly thing he did to you only reflects that he had missed his father.

BRANDON
> What about me, Aunt? Well, I will have to, I suppose. This is the last time, Aunt Maud, that I'm going to do it—forgive him. The next time, I'm gonna bloody his nose, Aunt as we use to and give him a good hiding like when we were boys growing up.

"At that time, we made up, only for the shithouse to do it again."

The taxi driver was waiting. His name was taken from his badge ID.

ARNOLD GRISLY (DRIVER)
> What you're going over there for, stranger?

"He asked this inquisitively after I told him where I was going."

ARNOLD GRISLY (DRIVER)
Stranger, there's nothing over there beside darkness and ghost.

BRANDON
Yes. These parts. Pi, you know. One of my friends is living over Palm Road. Know it? And my name's Brandon Willows.

ARNOLD
That entire area's derelict for some years now; councils moved the people out a there long time ago. Your friend's given you the wrong address. There was promise to rebuild that place back, but I guessed they've run out of money. No, mate. No one living there for years now. Still want to go?

BRANDON
Can't see why I should come this far and not see the place.

ARNOLD
Well, want to see for yourself, eh?

BRANDON
Damn sure, I want to. Yes, I do. A tourist attraction for me.

ARNOLD
Kind of from the council. You're not a spy, are you? Could spot you a mile off? See, me chaps down at London send spies out 'round places like here to have access on what's going on up this end. Now, tell me that you're one. Need something to happen 'round here?

"He bemoaned as the vehicles travelled along and disappeared into black shadowy mist. It just turned into the early hours of the morning."

BRANDON
Need something to happen round these parts, right?

"Shank had been recently spending more time around prison, or somewhere in the vicinity, than elsewhere. I considered it a path neither she nor I wanted. But that's life; it would send you down or up the tube before you realized it—post pomposity.
"Arnold was one of those cabbies that one could grow to like. He talked and responded to questions about the places, well, up on geography of England and from the Saxon to its orientation of the present day. Then, half an hour later, it became boring and sort of intricate to follow. Nonetheless, he was still a good guy."

ARNOLD
Put a word in for us when you got back. Don't paint us all red. Believe me, mate, lots of ghosts in these parts. Can't see any humans around? That's the place you're looking for.

"He pointed to three terrace-like buildings."

ARNOLD
Not goin' to leave you round here on your own, boss man.

BRANDON
Stick around for a bit, why don't you.

"The diesel engine gurgled lowly as the head beam levelled off and focused onto the door marked '21.' I then walked up a step or two, curled my index finger, hit the wood with the wedding ring, and listen for life form. I did it for a second. Then, there was sound of humans coming.

ARNOLD
Anything?

BRANDON
Life's around, it seems.

FRITZ
Bran? What you're doing here? Sorry, can't invite you in.

"I needed to change my lungs before I could answer, and when the door was opened, I needed a larger mouthful of fresh air that would save me from methane poisoning."

BRANDON
No. Unless a doctor is around to administer heart, lungs, and kidney transfer on the spot, you're going to die, Fritz. So, this is where you're nesting out. A bird has a better place than this.

ARNOLD (*shouting*)
Good heaven! If someone did tell me, I wouldn't believe it!

BRANDON
So, that's where you and Borer trump up your little organization for muscling in on us?

FRITZ

Don't think the worst of me, Bran. I'll get some pants on and come out to you. Wait a minute for me, old chap.

"Something remained fishy, but it was his life, or the style, he subjected himself to."

BRANDON

As your boss would say—none of my business.

FRITZ

Is this a third-degree inquest? Is that what you came for? Mow, Brandon is here.

BRANDON

Far more than that is what I want to know.

"Other vehicle headlights hit the misty morning spread. It was my driver who noticed and alerted us of the awareness campaign. Those headlights lighted up the place like beacon searchlights in the darkness."

ARNOLD

A bit busier around here.

"He loudly acclaimed it. Fritz came running from the terrace house with his hand stuck inside one of his shirtsleeves. He had a key ring in his mouth, and he managed to tumble with both feet halfway through his trousers. He could have been a big bumblebee that had lost one of its wings. Had that scene been a part of the film *Paint Your Wagon*, then we would have been the extras in that movie, except we were taking early morning doses. Mow came out, too, with all of her belongings in her hand and had just managed to slide into the vehicle as we did."

FRITZ (*to taxi driver*)

Get going. You better get out a here fast, my friend. He was talking to the taxi driver.

"We had just circled inside the estate's perimeter when there came several flashes of lights that heavily contained reminders to Fritz that he was playing a naughty game with whoever they were. The greater force of gelignite on the human's ears both remained with explosives of envious tenacity and were as dangerous as glycerine when mixed."

FRITZ

Did you set me up, Bran?

BRANDON

No, Fritz. I would've done it better. That must be Borer's men. I just want to get to the bottom of you and Borer's nests. Set Shank up, didn't you?

FRITZ

Don't be stupid, old boy. They must have followed you in. Given notice for sometime now that they would becoming Nasty.

"I ordered the cab driver to drop him off at the next crossroad. It was then when he insisted that he would pay the cabby to take him to another camp ten miles away. He was annoyingly subdued. He was a chameleon-type of human—touches the sky when he feels like it, yet in that same moments was in hell tucking away."

BRANDON

Nothing to say, Fritz?

FRITZ

A lot to say, Bran. But you know how it goes, old boy. Just can't spill too much. One thing, I know too little, and too much of a kind. Can go either way.

BRANDON

These guys just blow your nest apart, and you're so damn calm. I'd be over there with a few grenades and my blowtorch with my RPG to complete that lot. Only got guts for your family?

Chapter Eight

FRITZ
> Even though you're having a child on the way?

BRANDON
> What the hell you're talking about? Men don't have babies. Not yet, and don't see how they will. Would be a lost race and sterile anyway. Are you telling me that you're going to....

"Fritz's face drooped a little. Then he raised his head and smiled."

FRITZ
> You damn ghettos' rat. Didn't she tell you?

BRANDON
> Who—when—what?

FRITZ
> Shank's having a baby. That has put you in a far comprising situation more than you will want to.

Later...

BRANDON
> Shank! Why? When did she tell you all this? I don't believe it.

FRITZ
> She's going to tell you tonight. Guess she didn't make it. But you're going to be a daddy.

BRANDON

    And she's in jail? You put her there for all I know!

FRITZ

    Don't worry. Mow is looking out for her. She'll be free soon—when you agree that Mow is coming in on Borer and the department's behalf. Resist it, and your business will cease. Rapped up. Finish. Caput.

"The taxi reached their chosen spot, and Fritz and Mow were dropped off at this designated location. Then I went off to catch a train with tepidity. Meanwhile, after my encounter with Fritz, Steve acclaimed to us that he would be coming back early the next day since somehow, Shank put up his bail. I need to be thinking while riding back on the train. Who was trying to blow Fritz away and for what purpose? I owed Aunt Maud that favour to finding out.

"I suspected that Borer's department had something to do with our present crisis. I contacted him before I went and saw Shank who was released on bail to appear before the magistrate court on a yet to be fixed date. By now, she'd been released into Mow's care. I'd asked Borer not to drive, and I wouldn't either for the obvious reason and sake of laying the prescription camouflage ahead. Later, Borer was sitting at a rounded table when I got there, holding a glass of fresh stream water."

BRANDON

    Our little boy, Fritz, knew about these things before they'd happened. Even knew of my wife's pregnancy before I did. Can you say how?

BORER

    Dunno what you're talking about, Willows. If I did want to set you up, my lad, I'd done it a while back. And another thing: Why would I want to take you out?

BRANDON

    Not sure. How about someone's pissing on you about us, a mean putting on some pressures? Or some of those who'd lost out seeking revenge. What would you do then? Could be that our ethnic background are the cause.

"Borer seemed a bit surprise, taping out his own PBX with the index. However, I had to find where the storage of the glycerine, gelignite, and other resources were, where the kegs were stored and coming from or waiting to blow us out at anytime. Because I think then that Guy Fawkes were still playing bout with gunpowder."

BRANDON
The shithouse smell. Lots of gas about, methane inspectors.

"Borer didn't reply, but knowing him, he'd just dropped his mind in the slots of overtime. He leant forward."

BORER
Somehow, the message got around. I heard it, too, from my upper echelons, but they don't know that you or your firm is involved. So stay that way. Will keep you there as long as I have to.

BRANDON
Won't take long for some gutter rats to put two and two together? And what then?

"The reply he gave was reassuring on the one hand but uncertain on the other."

BORER
When we reach the bridge, we cross.

BRANDON
Pause. When you got there, someone blows the bridge. What then?

BORER
Then it would be time to rebuild it or build another around it, above it, under it, or aside. Couldn't be better, savvy?

BRANDON
Get your drift, DIB.

"Shank just started dinner when I got home. She stood at the sink, putting along her George Foreman smile. I gave her a peck and tried to smooth things."

BRANDON
Setting up something at the stock? Need another excuse to flush out any rats there? Linking in BAID having nothing' to say, doll—it means to tell me.

SHANK
Fritz again. What's wrong with men?

BRANDON

I don't know what's wrong with men, doll. Tell me? I think I should be the first to know. I'm glad, happy, and rejoicing. But I still want to know why you've got to let that creepy son of a bitch in my life. The guy's a waste.

SHANK

You're tired, darling. Have some rest. We'll talk when you calm down or get off your high horse.

BRANDON

Yeah, don't want the ticker to stop going.

"Shank's own collection was gathering dust, but the cheque continues to roll in, although she was now unable to fulfil her own matrimonial investigation. I visited Steve regularly; his case was pulse star-like. I had suspected that he might somehow be right about the higher-up's involvement. Earlier, I furthered my navigation with Shank and had accessed her views."

SHANK

Sure, we don't want that to happen before he comes along to carry on with the business, do we? Never seen her, and her Steptoe and Sons is a classic piece presenting male chauvinistic, adult-centred, manipulation double standard dribble.

BRANDON

Have the centre's dish for lunch today, hon. So, why don't you cool it and let me dig that piece of moronic tube you're wearing, commonly known as head-dig? Why don't you just let me in to salvage a small screw from that tube? Your views on Steve? Still got a few grand left after your motor repair?

"Shank, pre-emptive of what she'd been doing, came and sat, still wearing her pinafore and oven gloves.

SHANK

Shouldn't do that when I'm cooking. Mow was saying something today about...Steve.

BRANDON

Time we see a good lawyer for the poor bastard. Think he's entitled to legal aid? Can't tell how much worth he has under his bonnet. Can't be the lottery that turned him into an overnight millionaire or something, so it must be the horse or it's the pool. Wouldn't turn him into megabucks, but would be enough. Let's say he's worth a hundred Gs'. We had twelve and a half G. That left him with a cool eighty-seven G, plus interests. Nothing touches. Talk to him today. By this time, he probably got some further info and leads from Mow.

SHANK
Will do.

"After dinner that evening, I tried to visit Steve at the local station. However, he hadn't been in for a while. I heard he was moved some thirty miles away with restricted visitors; Shank and I were excluded from the list. The next day, I went to consult a firm of solicitors recommended by the law society."

Later that afternoon...

DUPONT
Friend or family?

Chapter Nine

BRANDON
Client.

"I then related what we have come to understand as issues of the case."

DUPONT
Know who was the judge at his trial or who legally represented him at his trial then?

BRANDON
Can get that for you.

"DuPont was taking notes. He looked at me through the level of his bi-focals inquisitively. He was articulate in his delivery and adjudged that he might have been some prison officer or the unlit saboteur of justice."

DUPONT
It is going to cost. If what you're saying is right, it looks as if it's already been tied up. Only leaves the preliminaries and formalities. If that's the case, it's already decided upon, only to be proceeded by a judge. Could be tough.

"He turned to the phone on his desk. I heard he asked for information about Steve, but he was put on hold. He dialled again and was put on hold again. Fifteen minutes had gone when he put back the phone on its hook. He commenced to enlarge the scenarios."

DUPONT
All the stages must have been completed, or your client is a danger to other people or to himself. Else, if he's not, then he is in relatively deep

trouble with a charge of attempted murder hanging over his head. May not get off scot-free. See what I can do. I'll get a court list to see when he will be back in court. It may take some time, but I'll dig it up somehow.

"When I left the solicitor's office and returned to my office, DuPont already telephoned and left a message with Mow. I had just entered the office. It was evening."

MOW

The inspector wants you to call him straight away and the solicitor you've seen today wanted you to ring him. Tries to get you unsuccessfully on the mobile.

BRANDON

Who would you say is more urgent, Mow? Always have women in my life. My mum was one.

"Mow looked at me from the office, the type that'd made it accessible for others to find out things—corporate espionage. That rings a bell. I surmised that she already relayed to Borer the details of DuPont's communication in so many words."

MOW

The inspector, of course, Sir.

"I did as Mow requested. I'd suspected that the inspector would be blowing dragons, but he didn't. His tone was cool, kind, and placid on the phone, almost sounding dangerous. I preferred when he's in his wearing outfits. Meanwhile, at Borer's office a day later, in the morning..."

BORER

How's Shank?

"Then I knew that something was wrong. I was unsure if I should ask him what it was about."

BORER

Got a little surprise for you, Willows. Must say I surprised myself. Going with the job you're currently avoiding? Savage's having a party at his country place; I can't make it. So do it for me, will you? Take Shank. This invitation is for both of you. While you're there, see if you can pick anything. Not telling you to spy; keep your ears to the ground. Let me know how you get on, will you?
"I didn't reply affirmatively."

BRANDON

Don't know if I am going to make it. But for your sake, I'll try my utmost, DIB.

"His grin was resident and native as those worn by mosquito seeing blood for the first time."

BORER

What whether? By the way, Fritz will be there. I advise you not to make contact with him, at all, if it can be helped.

BRANDON

Like louse in the head. Thanks for letting me know.

BORER

Thought it's a good idea to warn you of his presence. Look out for him as well. Double crossed you before. Won't see why he would resist it again.

"Yes, that advice was a clear cut, probably aside from the old cat grin he wore for security. However, I had to wonder whether he had slipped a bit in for himself. When I left for the door after half an hour, he was in state of jubilation. I left uncomfortable bearing his instruction. No policeman was ever happy—not in my book. Later, when I returned to the office, DuPont telephoned again. Steve's case was moved to Lincoln, some hundred miles away. He would be sitting for the next morning."

BRANDON

If Alice is in Wonderland, then this is it. I'm in there with her right now.

"I reminded myself: Shank wasn't going to be at the office. Her pockets of plan fall at her post-maternity examination. A letter addressed to me arrived from the West Indies, which I had slipped unread into my pocket. There's no better time than any to open the script screwed up envelop by then. DuPont was on the other line, knocking my brain about with legality, that of the 'if' things. 'Do the jobs and do it cool, man.' That's how Steve would have said it."

DUPONT

His legal aid is only a preliminary green form type; won't cover my fees. Need a cheque for £5,000 right away. Can you manage that much? I have to go there in the morning. With that, I do not have to travel down to Lincoln. I'll get a colleague to do the representation in court, but I would like to see the colour of his money before I can move.

BRANDON
What's his chance and what he's getting out of that?

DuPont
Right now, I won't try to give you any hope of a bail. From this angle, Mr. Willows, it seems crazy to me.

"I began to browse the script addressed to me from the West Indies."

BRANDON
I think what Steve's been saying all along has some bearings.

DuPont
Could have done?

BRANDON
Get you the cheque in a minute.

"I was certain that Mow has been listening when I'd finished speaking with DuPont. His line was clear when I browsed through the script, still haggling with the mouthpiece. One thing was happening well for me, reading between the lines. Reading. *Dear Brandon, Why did you never tell me that the woman was mad? The woman is mad! One minute, she's going to marry me, and another minute, she's hostile. When it's again on me, will send you a letter, come, and let you know. You might have to fly out overnight. Give me love to Shank. Long to see you all. Come back soon. Love I, Jupt.*
"It couldn't be at a better time. I started humming a tune that my memory had thrown out."

BRANDON (STANDING UP, WINDING AND SINGING)
Come along now, everybody. Come and hear what I have to say, for in every corner where I walk, I see a group of people parks. They're not skylarking; they're only talking about Ethiopia.

MOW
What's that you're...?

BRANDON
Never mind that, Mow. This is a native song I picked from the West Indies where we were before. That was rumba and mentor classics as they call it. The return to Ethiopia song, man.

MOW
Sure. Talk to Dick already?

"The office door opened, and Shank walked in."

SHANK
What's happening here?

MOW
He's happy.

BRANDON
No, I'm not just happy.; I'm ecstatic. Shank, doll, he's not going to get married to whom he was going to marry. Don't you see? It's off!

"I handed her the script."

BRANDON
Tell me about what they're saying about the little fella. Now, I can give to Steve some reasonable attention.

"The two women looked at me disturbingly."

SHANK
Borer was talking about that. Steve's case, I mean.

BRANDON
Sure. What did he say to dramatize it further? Get Fritz for me, Mow.

"It was a week later when Steve supplied us with information. Shank and I attended Savage's party. It was upmarket stuff. The spreads were out of bounds for ordinary humans. It was such a night."

SHANK
This is hot stuff.

"As we stood viewing our surroundings, the champagne trays had moved towards us as though they were on celestial chariots. We had introduced ourselves separately. As soon as we were introduced, I grabbed one of the glasses."

BRANDON
Yeah, I can smell that, son. Know anyone here?

Chapter Ten

"Shank put her index across my lip succinctly, hinting of what she reminded me earlier. Without any word said, we smiled our way to the dance floor and people watched us dance. Soon, I wangled my index to her pulse and found it was there, waiting and pulsating as much. We got out and got home. It was weekend, and that little boy would be well fed. It was the following day when we decided to invite ourselves back on the dance floor at the Savaggy den. For the following weekend, we were supposed to be invited.

"That week, we were sizing up what we would be looking for about their company when we returned. The weekdays passed quite quickly, and before time, we were back, sipping from those expensive glasses that only the rich and famous could have drank from and afford. We got to the dance floor. There, the band was playing a mixture of waltz that changed quickly to the Cha-cha melodies. My nephew who taught us to dance salsa could not have done a better job. A few of the older gentlemen who were standing and sipping from their glassed, aroused by their female partners, pressed into service. They were being led like sheep to be slaughtered, in our case, dance to the melodies. I could understand why, but I might not get used to the real agolance had I been there for other reasons.

"Since I have known Shank, she socially mixed with all my friends, particularly those that I mostly care for, including relatives. I had considered that Borer was sort of a good man, but this mixing with people, coming by leaps, I barely have time for. The suspect of Shank who was not lively enough for their liking as to us the newcomers and who could plainly set off issues, according to Steve—'big problems.'"

BRANDON
One can't clean the pond and escape being wet; it's natural.

SHANK
Pooh! That's the way they grab you down under the water, slowly take you over, and get you to do the things they do. Can't grumble anymore?

"It was suitable for the purpose —an upmarket setting. The large house sat in a wide verdant field like a duck swims in a lake. The fortification was by a trench dugout with suitable metal lattices. It served as a bridge across the trench allowed our vehicles access to the house. It had a few humps that might turn a vehicle on its side if moving at fast speed. There was a small gate that opened automatically. From there, a thin wire line stretched along and winded back to the other side, forming a complete circuit. It seemed certain to me that any human who would fall into the trenches would not come out alive. Shank and I were not there for crackpots trying to sharpen their carpals on any of us for sure. The fine decor of the building assured that it had gone through durable times before Savaggy got a hold of it."

SHANK
'Bout how much he paid for this?

BRANDON
How much chairman got today? Something like 400 Gs or maybe more.

"Nobody seemed to be bothered any longer—no worries of intruders, thieves, or any mayhem that might shatter the evening's enjoyment. Gentry were posted along the entrances, and from peepholes, I had glimpsed them slowly walking about. There was total security, I observed.
"I started to mix some coffee and milk; honey would be coming later. At the moment, it was satisfactory for continuously sailing my way, with the stops and rests and with my two antennas prolonged to listen to some enlightening gossips. My reliance was solely left to the assumptions of the criminal mind to search and, documented the information correctly to the memory."

SHANK
Savaggy' wife is beautiful, isn't she?

BRANDON
Yeah. Not as much as you, though.

"That was the signal to split. Shank went toward Mrs. Savaggy while I snarled, crossing paths as the tender music played. Classic music was slowly played by the band. It was then that I noticed Shank dancing away with Savaggy. I knew she would soon get in the environment; I'd come to expect it. Continuing my circulation amongst the guests, I noticed there was Fritz, in smart, upmarket attire, too. In my book, though, he remained a chameleon of sort who preferred to avoid everything when possible. I walked over to him, reminding myself of Borer's instructions. What he had in mind, I did not know and I was not a mind reader. Borer would not divulge what he was aiming to achieve from Shank and me. If it was to achieve a good social climate with Savaggy, then we had succeeded without a bullet being fired. But if he sent us there to spy and report, I would say there were ample suspects in those confines. Where the carcass is, there will be the vultures.

"On the other hand, if it was for information-gathering, I could see that it was freely available and everybody was suspect. Shank was to remember the female names and look into their lifestyles. I was going to do the same; I would memorise the male-driven environment and their lifestyles. We were to compare notes from memory when we got back home. It was midnight when we were about to leave. Savaggy and his wife were told that we were going; They came to bid us farewell. The pleasant evening had come almost to its end."

SAVAGGY
    Enjoyed it?

SHANK
    Enormously so.

"Mrs. Savaggy took Shank by the arm, and they walked away. They were talking and smiling at each other as though they had met before. This left Savaggy and me alone; we could freely exchange a few simple words."

SHANK
    Nice people.

MRS. SAVAGGY
    Seen anybody you know?

SHANK
    Should I?

MRS. SAVAGGY
    How about him?

"She pointed at Fritz whose back was turned toward us."

SHANK
    Don't spoil the evening, Mrs. Savaggy. I came to listen to Caesar's, not to bury him. Don't spoil it. I must say you've thrown a good party, and I enjoyed it.

MRS. SAVAGGY
    Hope you'll come again.

Chapter Eleven

SHANK
> Don't bet on it. I might. I might not. It depends.

MRS. SAVAGGY
> Hear me out please, Mr.s Willows. The party was for social interaction. They're my friends who invited me to their social get-together. I just did. Besides, for one to get truly in society, one got to interact. And May— that's my husband—doesn't get about much socially.

In the meantime…

SAVAGGY
> Seems mine and your wife hit it off. I would like her to have friends, social friends, Mr. Willows.

SHANK
> Hanging out your responsibilities to someone else? It's a cad game?

"Shank returned, and we made our way back home. Before sleeping, we compiled files of each person present in Savage's party. We compiled them by name, address, nature, disposition, and lifestyle. We reminisced what went on during the evening."

BRANDON
> Don't any of these lots know who you are, Fritz?

FRITZ
> Whisperings could say that I don't know you. Keep away. See that one over there?

"He beckoned with a sort of chinned-up nod."

FRITZ
That's the man you've been looking for, isn't he? One in the tinted.

BRANDON
Pooh! Who is he? Industrial or plain saboteur?

FRITZ
Looking for Massey, aren't you?

BRANDON
Nothing escapes you, is there?

FRITZ
Blood's thicker than water, if you get my drift. I'm after the one he's talking with. Should've killed the bastard when I got the chance.

BRANDON
Both are sharks?

FRITZ
Leads you to the bigger ones. They just carry out the dirty works. Work for the big bastards—banks and other big institutions.

"We flew from the scene just after midnight and, as promised, compared notes. There was nothing other than the usual social activities and suspects and other than Massey who was certainly aware of our presence. Whether he knew what we were after or not, we would soon know on our table the following morning.

"A car pulled up outside our office the next morning: it was Massey. The driver only in his vehicle. He too had his hair dyed jet black. Contrary to his age, he dressed following that of an eighteen-year-old's style. I could see he had worn a toupee which made him look like a younger rooster where in fact, he was over fifty. Some damn old cock-a-doodle-doos do when in late fifties. Massey seemed to know more about our operations when he came along. Knowing, he, too, came to pry, maybe about what we knew of him or to tell us that the sharks needed cleaning or the pond was getting murky. However, he was there for other reason than I at first thought."

BRANDON
Mi.... I know you'd be here. Mr. Massey?

MASSEY
Don't know if you do, but if not, you may be missing the action.

"He became stern."

MASSEY

For instance, by Providence, I happen to associate with a person whom there was hardly anything about him known for some time, a special person.

BRANDON

Meaning?

"He held the briefcase case on his lap tightly. I urged him to carry on."

MASSEY

Are you a judge, barrister, or what? If you're any of those, you are corrupt to the health. But Satan will have you for breakfast before you even fade from this life.

RENE MASSEY

I gather information for the judiciary. Advice and plan. Say, like a non-governmental body, but governmental body in a sense.

BRANDON

Operates outside the law when you want to and in when it suits you best?

RENE

Probably true. That's why I could not stop in the hospital or let your chap understand the problem. Cloak and dagger, so to speak.

BRANDON

You're going to send him down, aren't you? Or stand aside and see that poor bastard being sent down again?

RENE

A little piece of free advice, Mr. Willows.

"He stood up from the chair and rested the handheld case, which he was holding by the middle handle, onto the desk."

BRANDON

Just a minute. I stood for no threat—none at all. So don't you hear telling me in your capacity what I didn't ask you. What I do want to know, though: Are you the one pushing for Steve to be sent down?

"Mow had just left for lunch, leaving Shank who had been yawning all morning in the office."

RENE MASSEY

Security, Mr. Willows. Let's say his wife's part of the organization. But the lad's behaviour needs to be desisted; needs calming down a bit.

BRANDON

So, you're teaching him a lesson or two. Is that the case? Knocking off his wife while he's away and now trying to get him back in?

RENE MASSEY

About right, Mr. Willows. He's not alone in there. My son is in there, too, you know.

BRANDON

Same reason, I suspect? Knocking off his miss as well, hmm?

RENE MASSEY

Might have. He's in there for something more serious than Steve's case. Steve was sent in to find out who was the main man behind the cartel syndicate who wanted the prototype, seemed well-versed, and put out for BAID industry from my son. Your boss, Borer, knows all about it; he's been briefed.

BRANDON

Had I been your son, I would have committed your head in the sewer, you damn dog. He didn't get it, so you're sending him back? Is that the case?

Chapter Twelve

RENE MASSEY
Hmm. He'll get it this time. I'm sure he's capable of rendering himself useful, Mr. Willows. And now that I have taken the trouble to enlighten you, please withdraw from the case all together and let it run its course. Treat it as a man-to-man favour.

BRANDON
Or else?

"The obstacle course had just been set up. How, where, and what it was about, we were going to find out."

SHANK
What you're thinking, darling?

"After Massey left, Shank and I discussed the course that we might take. We would not be taken out of bounds by Mow who had been on her lunch. She was noted to be constantly talking with Fritz, not good combination after what had occurred previously to this operation."

SHANK
Steve's in a hook, but he must have known what he was getting into.

BRANDON
Think the poor bastard might know, but under great pressure, he might have given in.

SHANK
Remember Borer talking of thieves to cork another? Same pot we're in, hon.

BRANDON
Could be that we're in circles of crooks. That what you're saying, doll?
Sugar!

"Mow returned a little earlier and sat down, reading the daily broadsheet's economic column which was in large print."

MOW
BAID being referred to the M.M.C.

BRANDON
Who's the writer of that article, Mow? Please find out who he is and get him for me—the editor, the headman, or the chief, if possible.

MOW
I'll do that.

"She took the page and went down the article. Then she handed it over her shoulder. They had set up an inquiry to respond to a question from an MP (Minister in the House of Parliament) about the whole affairs of BAID and its working relationship. It was held as the minister agreed that there would be an in-depth inquiry relating to the complaint received of insider dealing which was already on the M.M.C. table. The prototype developments of the aircraft destined to serve twenty-first century passengers had been troubled since the revelation of its aptitude and manoeuvrability. It was stressed that there was no concrete evidence that the rumours regarding a cartel dealing to delay or hijack the prototype was true. Another MP asked if there were sufficient funds for the aircraft's development. The ministers declined to answer it."

BRANDON
This is the bit we want.

"It was true that the new aircraft would be using nuclear fusion as fuel, which would enable the aircraft to fly at a speed that was unthinkable just a decade or so ago. However, the drawback was that it would be flying over cities with human cargo. The threat of accidents must be considered as humanists were in a fury."

BRANDON
If they say it, it isn't true.

MOW
Bet your bottom dollar it is.

SHANK
Who are they trying to fool?

MOW
The public, of course. It's not as if they could just tell the truth as it is.

"She pondered. Accordingly, all of the three active lines were peaking."

MOW (*talking to Borer*)
See the paper today, Sir?

BORER
As a matter of fact, I haven't. In normal routine, I just glimpse through them. To read all the papers in the office is a full time job. You should know that, Mow. What is it you're asking me to look at?

SHANK
The economic page, Sir. Most of them carry the same heading on page six today. See it, Sir? Mr. Willows wanted a word on whether it is a joint venture among the Americans, the British and the Europeans, Sir.

"Angle from an insider's view: There was a smartly-dressed, elderly man who rang the attention bell. He handed in a parcel to the receptionist at BAID for Mr. D/S. Then he left in an M3 Jag. Fritz's blue Ford saloon had been seen parked earlier, a little distant from BAID's entrance. His car seemed to have broken down. He went to the reception and asked for water. The parcel was still lying on the counter, he noticed. He left shortly with a bottle of water given by the receptionist.
"He scrawled on his calendar for Massey's number and linked his telephone to Nula."

BRANDON (*on the phone*)
I'm trying to trace this motor's registration. It is possible you could give the name of the owner who ran into me and just shot off? It's for the insurance purposes.

DVLA (*Driver and Vehicle Licensing Agency, three-way telephone conversation with Borer*)
It's on a company-registered fleet, Sir. This particular number is marked none disclosure. Maybe you have to go through your insurance to obtain it. But I'm afraid we can't help you any further, Sir.

BORER
Is it a BAID registration? Can you say at yes or no?

DVLA

Yes—I mean no, Sir. See, Sir, it's under the Disclosure Act. I can't help you any further, Sir.

BORER

Damn disclosure; it impedes everything. To answer your question about the collaboration to build the aircraft, the main players are Americans, British, Europeans, and the Russians. Is that answering your query, Willows?

"He put away the phone."

Chapter Thirteen

"I was in a queue. Fritz showed up later with Borer who was leading the operation. They'd come together from a meeting. By then, there was a clear distinction regarding who the suspect and who the insiders were. However, hiding from their conspicuous looks proved to be more difficult; it was only from physical amplification that they could bring themselves into the open as was agreed. From the breed of similar jag, it was agreed not to carry out physical harm to the vehicle if things did go as planned, but it didn't because someone has been doubling up their characteristic from the inside. In the limo, Borer and Savaggy briefly discussed the danger. Then it was afternoon."

SHANK

Think it's possible for someone to arbitrate a takeover of their industry? And suppose that that happens, who takes over then? They might move it out of our control and then sell the aircraft to the Al-Qaeda in lock, stock, and barrel.

BRANDON

Oh, doll! That's been the case often. Firms in trouble, someone burns the place down. Insurance pays, guy who owns it is back in business, and the public's none the wiser. When it happens, bet your bottom dollar that none of the officer's tool is involved *because they can account for every step when the fire was on*. Out of the way they are. And when they do that, neither my son nor anybody else can kiss their arse good-bye before the fallout of uranium over any city if one of those crafts goes down over it or even nearby.

MOW

How'd they get away with it? I like this business.

"Shank smiled when she handed me a parcel. I handed her a box of chock let. It equalled to an exchange; no robbery had been intended."

SHANK

You do. Start to churn the sludgy parts. Don't forget; they'll swallow you in one big gulp.

"After dinner that evening, I tried to visit Steve at the local prison. But he'd been moved some thirty miles away and visitors were restricted. Shank and I were included on the list of restricted persons. It was two weeks later when I visited the solicitor on Steve's behalf."

DUPONT

Of course, Mr. Willow. I say if it has anything to do with government departments, it is unlikely to win, unless, of course, you laid hold on the streets, with banners and all that stuff. Can't get a dickybird from any department about your client? I did inform you that from what you told me, the trials are only preliminary, dealing with the normal run of the mill thing.

"DuPont stared across from his bifocals."

DUPONT

You don't think he was mixed up with any other elements, do you Mr. Willows?

"I didn't reply to his inquiry immediately."

DUPONT

Mr. Willows, do you know of anything that might give him a chance? If none, then I can't go on any further. Unless something comes up early, he will be going down—for some time, I strongly suspect. Why did you take on this case? Must be from desperation?

"He did not wait for me to reply and clarify before he asked."

BRANDON

Shouldn't say too much, but yes, I think he's involved in something far bigger than how he sees it. A proposition was put before him in an either or either— a mode which he takes on a job that if could not be delivered, he may as well go down. Maybe better for him to do so; better chance, maybe the only way. Probably, it is inevitable.

DUPONT

Why haven't I been told of this when you came along at first?

BRANDON

Didn't know you want to. Still under investigation. And believe me, a lot of muddy, slime-soup sludge's been coming up.

"My mobile interrupted our conversation."

MOW

"I'll do it right away. Ever do works for BAID?"

Why do you ask?

BRANDON

Matter of elimination.

MOW

BAID.

"He was pondering."

I remember reading they are developing a world-beater aircraft for the twenty-first century travellers. What do you want to know about it? Saw a little piece about the firm being referred to the M.M.C., noting that it is suspected of an insider dealing. What you think?

SHANK

Can't say for sure. Could be.

"I went to see Borer at the closing of the week to have one of our sessions. Neither Mow nor Shank was there. It was evening. I'd no choice of choosing my enemy; Fritz was there. He smelled a little bit better than when I saw him just before his nest was ironically blown up. I related to Borer that Steve and Massey were lying in the same nest, outside of his woman being in bed with Massey."

BRANDON

Only that the bigger bird pushed the smaller one out of it. Probably, he is the bigger one lying. Shark.

BORER

Told you to leave it off, Willows.

"He begins and turns on his tapping on his desk he was looking somewhere else."

SHANK

But, DIB.... In the roll of the investigation, it seems you all are sitting in the same pogo, Sir. Is this an elementary at M.M.C. or another formality?

Fritz (*calling*)

Bran, you're getting paid for it. So what do you care about?

BORER

Be eating grass soon. Not careful, Mr. Willows. While I have my doubt about the whole affair, I'm coming up for my thirty years, going on pension and all that. Risky trying to help you or your kind.

BRANDON

So I can see now why you all want a little unknown firm to carry the can: no-good upstarts, with criminal background—who's going to know? Your big chap, Savaggy, maybe the one who's undermining his own nest or selling out to the cartel. No better one in the know-how more than he is, isn't it right, DIB?

FRITZ

Can't hang a man on assumption, Bran, can you?

BRANDON

And why not? The law hang a lot of innocent bloke on probability. You know that, don't you? And Steve is one of them. I want to move into BAID myself starting next week to do a bit of nosing about.

BORER

Too much exposure—can't allow that. But, Fritz, you can go in. In the security business, I can set it up for you. But first, we must create a situation to get you in there. What do you say, Willows?

"We stayed away from my office for that weekend setting up Fritz organization while I went on a one-man crusade to see who were tying up with whom.

"I went to the office early the following Monday morning; it has just tweaked the still darkish dawn. I put the key through the door when something dropped the other side. Mow wouldn't be in until late morning; she was excused as Fritz's partner. Shank was left in bed having one of her morning things.

"We considered Steve's case and his reliance on us to sort it out. In the morning, I had no reason to be quiet anymore. Who might have been dumber or stone-hardhead. A hand came up and pushed the door against my face. Huge, sixteen-stone shoulders moved up, rammed the door, and entered the building.

"It was then when I twisted my shoulder as a monitor rammed against it, and I bounced back onto a desk. Then, as I drew up again and threw my six-teen-stoner body weight against a small statue, a whiff of perfume ran across my nostril. By then, I held onto the object and zapped the light switch that re-vealed a female intruder. She gazed at me with the piercing eyes of a pauper. Though she'd want to bargain, she got nothing to bargain with at that moment."

BRANDON

Who are you? Come on now, sister. Better tell me who you are or what you're doing here in my office, breaking in and entering. I'm calling the cops.

"She didn't answer until I completed the first three digits of profanity. The woman was Steve's wife. I never met her before. However, from her state-ments, she was dead giveaway."

INTRUDER

Got some money for my man. I want it or some of it to get him a good lawyer.

BRANDON

Hello? I already did that. And who are you? How did you know I am holding something belonging to him, and why have you broken in our office?

INTRUDER

Check you out. Don't know how you get into this. Business. You're a damn rascal. Aren't you the bloke that ran off with some people's dash a few years ago and our fund?

BRANDON

That's none of your business. So you're the one Massey's screwing? Steve's wife, aren't you? It puzzles me always—human's behaviour.

"I stood looking directly at the woman. She looked back. She was dressed as though she had been dragged from the edges. However, with a little clean up and some dubbing, she would be a fine-looking female even though she was a mixed-up gal."

INTRUDER

Wasn't screwing me! Wouldn't let that animal go on top of me!

BRANDON

> Sure! Steve thinks otherwise. How do you know he's an animal if you weren't cohabiting? Strange!

"I looked down at my watch; the news would be along soon. I turned the button on the radio and waited."

BRANDON

> Tell me a little about yourself, if you care...Mrs. Boot? Since you won't be going anywhere until you do tell me something better than you're trying to say now.

"She nervously pulled a packet of cigarettes out from her coat."

BRANDON

> There are fire hazards; won't allow it. You're a grasser, aren't, you? You were grassing on your husband for the cops. Then, they would kind of be in-the-know when he is coming out of prison. You planned the whole thing. Small price to pay—to get beaten up by your husband—to send him straight back into prison with all that evidence and keep him in there for life.

Chapter Fourteen

MRS. BOOT

Got to do som'at. Swear on my mother's life never grassed on my friend or family. There's no job about it, and what's there is to share amongst friends and the shit streamers, the yuppies. Bastards like me can't get in-the-know. What I don't know what it mean anymore?

BRANDON

No, you don't.

"When she pulled a package out from her inner coat pocket, it revealed her identity, from the chain hanging around her neck. I didn't let her know at once, but it seemed that Mrs. Boot, whether she was in on the game or she was be-having to be a complete idiot, was alone; she was speaking not just about her-self. That meant she also included us as one of her idiots."

BRANDON

Senseless woman. When was it decided that my place is in line to be raided?

MRS. BOOT

Come now, Mr. Willows, nothing like that. You all in the same dirty pond, I guess. I decided on my own to do it because my husband eggs-up him-self with you and leaving me out—you see.

BRANDON

Your identity card tells me that you're D.sg. Boot, is it not? Steve knows who you are? Bet the poor sod hasn't a clue. Sending females on their own now, is it? Cops and all of that?

"When she gave me that certain information requested I'd run the test through my mind; she was allowed to go but had to keep silent, as though I knew nothing except what we already knew. She was also asked to keep in touch and communicate whenever she like. Then I rang and woke up Shank, and I told her what had happened. Pity, I did, because she was round like a shot.

"Meanwhile, Fritz pulled up outside. His prized security vehicle carried a logo looking like the stings of a honeybee and with the carrier message 'We Run to Keep You Running.' Thought he'd choose something like himself— an enemy of families and humans. Then it was morning."

BRANDON

Just been raided, but it's all right. As soon as you have any info, let me know. I like to prepare a case for the first hearing at M.M.C. Keep your eyes on Savaggy; he's the man who hired us. Check him out first in line.

FRITZ

Him. Only if we could know what was inside.

"He looked at me readily. Our old partnership revived, I put his old tricks on standby mode."

FRITZ

Can't tell why we ever split up, Bran.

BRANDON

Once bitten, twice shy, old boy, and this wonder woman appeared on the scene. Things are getting exciting around here, maybe for better or worse. Depends on how we get on from now. Don't forget: I didn't choose my enemy.

"It was three weeks later when things started to move along nicely. It was our sources who revealed that Savaggy, Massey, and some other well-known industrial hit men met at the International Air show. Later, they dined together, which lasted the whole duration of their stay at the venue. The information was a break, but something was missing—something linking it in with anything abnormal. It was a matter of protecting the case all over and a bit of mulling along."

Later that afternoon...

"Our informer was Borer's friend. He said he got to be told the still unproved truth; the facts were not absolute but it could relatively be so. Some industrialists set fire to the aircraft's developers' buildings while others seemed to have sabotaged them internally. Others set up external diplomatic demise on the business and forced it to self-destruct. However, whatever was happening, the prototype couldn't be bought or merged. That was part of WPIA briefs."

SHANK

It could get ugly—Front-Tronics-like people.

BRANDON

Very. He would know how to break it to him gently. Massey's hiding behind some other felonious crutches. We have got to flush him out.

"Shank and Fritz gave their blessings; Mow wasn't at the session. The terms were then called."

FRITZ

The raid on our place then the haphazard handling of Steve's case. Smells, isn't it, Bran?

"Fritz cocked his finger like a trigger mechanism of a default pistol."

STEVE

De man did preach in de prison that God doesn't deal with my problem like how me hood a like it. Just he says, that some billions awe. And if my problem cum in de Z-line, den I got a long time fey wait. Me understand that bit. Den, a how God a put all of de Black people in de Z column all de time? I ask him that.

BRANDON

What were his replies?

STEVE

He does not have any answer fey them things, questions. Dem too deep fey de preacher man. And look how it simply a fey de black man. Him a deal with deeps tings from him was born oppression! He says it's a mystery. Bulldozer did ask him the same question. He gives him de same answers, too. Su God a probably dealing with de X column now. We still have a long way to go because he a deal with the Y before him gets to us; Z is De last group.

"I got Borer on the telephone early Thursday morning. I knew he reached his office around or about eight thirty. That was if he wasn't called out on night duty to identify some poor bastards who'd got their heads shot off or their guts ripped out in some drug-related incident. Although lately, he seldom did it, if there was anything at all. I knew he had Dick Whitehall training. He was becoming a man of leisure due to forces of old age and forces of being a policeman. He gathered around him heavyweights, many of them being the knowledge that Shank and his grandson would be well looked after should I tripped out, even though she had been forced not to call him 'daddy' by Borer legit wife Mr.s Hamilton."

SHANK

Soon to be man of leisure. I would like my father to be like Borer, but then, I didn't know him. He must be somewhere, though I want to get you two on your way before I go. He continues to say it more often now than before—you think darling. Anyway I got the adoption but I still want to know my real father is.

BRANDON

He'd been saying so, few times more often than Normal. It seems certain that one day, it'll happen.

"Shank and I trusted Borer for so much. If any White man would see us through, it was he. He had this way to approach a gut matter. Even if he was forcing himself to obey the law of natural selection, he was particularly calm. We suspect that Whitehall was not the sort of White man who missed anything. He was younger than I was, but his behaviour showed someone older than Borer and ambitious. Had he got the chance, Borer would be doing counter duty; it was only because of the pensioner's seniority that he hadn't. It went a long way."

Chapter Fifteen

"We were almost negatively certain that Whitehall would be pushing for total control on the outside contractors. Soon, if Borer stood in his way, he might roll across him as much. His flamboyant style riled Shank. I got the itches about how he was going about those procedures for our investigation reports, too. Right now, we had totally depended on Borer's cleanliness with our papers and all. However, I would like things to be straightened out so I might start working things for us including Frank who we think was there to pick up fallen bones off Borer Hamilton. Whitehall and I could get along, but with Shank, it was different. She had deep reservation about the suckers that were being lined up to sink Borer, her unclaimed father, who had given us too much rein in the secret society."

BRANDON
Pooh! Get a small unknown firm in and then give them the run around.

"I said it straight from the heart to the policeman."

BRANDON
And then make it known that an investigation's being done undercover. We're going to spit on those shitting, absurd buddies of yours.

"I met Borer the following day again at a meeting; it was to discuss our presumption. However, when the cops heard of it, he wouldn't move on. He promised to remove us from the case, but unknown to him, his reluctant behaviour was already plotted along our feelings. That meant we're becoming puppets instead of having full authority as promised."

BORER

> That's what you want? To make me look silly? When you gentlemen get back into the crime world, the public would say, "They tell us so." Keep your nose clean and you'll be all right.

"He nodded with a few disapproving ups and downs and then sideways which do not clearly tell us way how we should go or what we would do if his boss asked him now to resign, get back at us, and get us out the way following the juggling."

SHANK

> We did mention, if you recall, Sir, that we would be stirring up the pond. It meant that dust and grime would be getting into some animal eyes. We would be cleaning the big sharks, too. We might get eaten, but we made a promise to do our job.

BORER

> I've given you a job to keep you out of trouble and here you are being cleaner than clean.

SHANK

> We're not asking to bend your rules. No, not at all. Just reduce the intensity so we can get on with our part of the procedures. That's all. It's just that if one doesn't get washed sometime or another, they'll smell. Where's the water for the bent and dirty business people? Even just one time in their business lives or before they die, they should get a good scrub.

"Shank had driven her points home. Never seen her so straightforward with Borers who seemed to want us to turn the situation down to normal. He was like a father to her and all when he almost begged us to take on the job while considering what we might be able to turn up. That's what large firms do—curry favour and pay lip service like an obnoxious little boy who threw away his laxative pill."

BRANDON

> Pooh! And that's exactly how we expected it to be.

"In the arena, there seemed to be organizations within organizations operating as part of internal and external group for BAID jobs. We suspected that it came down from the higher-ups and filtered by a very few in the firm. Slowly but surely, the family was squeezed together, watching the corruption get greater automatically.

"The big fish remained in the bed at the bottom of the sea. They were camouflaged and was the cause of many problems (like getting to it and more than that, most importantly, flushing it out from amongst its protective skins).

The covering that it built around itself for customary protection was built from armour plating; nothing would be able to penetrate through it. Any armour-piercing tool would be too large for our operation, so we cleverly considered, since we did not have the tools required to do deep diving or to pierce its protective plating, to look for its most vulnerable spot to get through it.

"We were relying on Borer to help us with those tools of information already built up, but the policeman seemed to be having second thoughts, maybe his third. Who was to tell? Possibly, Whitehall was going over the file and Borer was becoming nervous.

"The policeman maybe, and very accurately, taking down statements, but he got to be called to interpret details more at any hearing. That was what we wanted from Policeman Borer, from the eyes that had seen those events—those little bits that were missing off the used A4s sheets in the filing basket.

"Fritz had gone in as security consultant to BAID. Mow came in earlier, on Wednesday morning, to finish off some papers. She was quite a technical-minded woman. That morning, she had worn a beautiful dress over her short and stubby self. Never seen something that matches as great. I thought one of those would suit Shank nicely when she had the baby. So, I asked where she got it from."

MOW
  Out of the catalogues—a new design. Like it?

BRANDON
  Suits you.

"I was embarrassed and then commenced to have thoughts—thoughts of what men think about women. Lots of blood rushed through me like a vampire seeing where its first meal was through the smell of blood. Not for me to tell the P. D. people what to wear, but it seemed strange. She had moved away from the usual black skirt and white blouse for that day."

SHANK
  Everybody knows that police people dressed in black of distinguishable sort. Black suits and the normal black socks, boots, and helmet matching with the department issues—a world pattern anywhere ones go.

BRANDON
  Just want a change, and Fritz's going to pick me up from here this evening. Have a guess who he's coming with.

"I knew in my mind then that that son of a bitch wasn't going be tamed. We got someone planted in the office; it was easy for him to make visits. Just after the morning post arrived, the telephone rang. Mow got at it. She was there, so there was no need for me to be in hurry to get calls."

MOW

Yes. This is Willows Private Investigation Associates. No, not association. He's here. You can speak to him. What bill? None that I know of, but you can.

"Mow was turning brilliant red when she handed the mouthpiece to me."

BRANDON

Willows here. How can I help?

VOICE (*calling from a hotel*)

This is Mount Pay Hotel and Resort.

BRANDON

Where is that?

VOICE

Well, you must have known where it is. You stopped here for a week and left without paying your bills, Sir.

BRANDON

You got to be kidding. Not me, my friend.

VOICE

Looking to receive your payments within seven days. This is an arrest able offence, Sir. You must send us your payments within the time specified as we're unable to find any credit arrangements for you or your company.

"The bastard put the phone down on me. Shank didn't feel well when she came to work that morning. Our boy was kicking the hell out of her all night. He had kicked me, too, a couple of times the day before. The unborn son of a bitch did when I tried to get to his mother. But I got outta that way fast since I'm not going to allow any child of mine to start kicking me before it was born. That's taking liberty; he had taken Shank away from me almost in total.

"Two months now, I haven't got any sex at all; even Mow would do from the office leisure's point of view, but I was considering Fritz who was supposed to be some sort of family. He had taken a couple of girls from my pasture. Now, it could be payback of dividends in kind. But then, my affairs would be called compulsory as it wouldn't be love in the sense.

"I commenced to notice Mow all day. That dress she was wearing was something. She had everything in it barring her face. Of course, when Shank's around, was strictly business. Had Mow in any way resembled anything near beautiful, I had some feelings that Shank would object on her working alone with me.

"Shank was on retention of the woman who engaged her to investigate her husband's foreign affairs. It was subjected in her divorce application proceedings. Every fifteenth day of each month, a cheque was placed on our accounts. That we followed up with a couple of phone calls to recheck if she was ready to continue her husband's overseas account. However, she put it on hold, observing if her husband to behave cleanly. Nonetheless, the cheques would continue to come."

Chapter Sixteen

SHANK

Unless I was asleep holidaying, it was preposterous for a hotel resort to ask us to pay a bill that wasn't incurred by WPIA.

BRANDON

Pooh! Musa, the H.M.P.S. looking for their cut?

"I was generalising around Shank and in Mow's presence. Up till now, things were going quite nicely. That was before Steve Boot and Borer Hamilton came into my life. I wished they did not, but their importance could not be overlooked. I came to realise that without both of the cases, each alone had a slim chance of being resolved."

MOW

Ever been to Wales, any of you?

"Still, I knew Shank hade some dealings in that neck of the woods. There were questions, though, that had to be asked for surety. I picked up this leaning at the court. The judge in the WPIA trial enlarged on his summing up."

JUDGE

Mr. Willows? You must be aware of your responsibilities toward the public and what your servants were doing at all times. I can't see how I can excuse you, taking your negligence into account. Therefore, I have no alternative but to sentence you for five years.

"Five years in the shutter. When the appeal failed Fritz, he turned into Crown Witness for the prosecution; it might have been a prisoner's dilemma. His sentence was reduced to eighteen months because his father had left home while two years were added on top of my five years."

FRITZ

No, not while I was there. You, Bran? HMPS don't send fraudster on holiday to Wales Hotel resorts. I never heard of it—absurd to ask. I would dismiss that even if it was true.

BORER

The taxpayers always look back for their cut. Feed, shelter, and clothe you for five years. Musa, worth something, Willows? And to make matters even worse, they give you little bit of pocket money. It goes a long way and added up at the end. Can't grumble. If they hadn't stuck their noses where they don't belong, then they wouldn't have to pick up our tab.

"DIB was government through and through. If he wasn't a policeman, then he would be a politico for sure, even a prime minister. Then, Shank and I would have no shitting chance of being reformed, trained, and now pursuing the PI game. The telephone rang shortly, and Shank picked it up. It had just gone after eleven. We hadn't yet sorted out the hotel file from our previous encounters. Shank turned her face away. I had expected it wasn't good. She had been listening intently, screwing up the phone coils."

SHANK

We didn't hire any car. No, no. We have no need for hiring any vehicle. Don't think that my husband did.

"She wasn't finish talking when I grabbed the mouthpiece."

BRANDON

Who are you, you son of a bitch?

VOICE

Think there's a mix-up here. Are you Mr. Brandon Willows?

BRANDON

Yes. Who's asking?

VOICE

My name is Slouch. Our car that you hired should've returned two weeks ago. We are trying to understand why the car hasn't returned. Might be you've decided to keep it longer and thought you would need to inform us. However, we have had no such arrangement. We would like you to return our vehicle or come in and let us deal with the problem.

BRANDON

Well, sorry to disappoint you, Mr. Slouch. I did not hire any car from you.

"He gave me the address. It was getting serious, and I had to go and see him. I arrived at the hire firm just tuning two-fifteen the same afternoon. I presumed Massey maybe playing his card. Fritz was slow to get off the ground. I made up a short report including our investigative findings and a summary. I prepared the surveillance for Borer's filing system although he probably wouldn't go along with our findings. He, too, became a protector of his friends and colleagues. Wrong or right, I commenced to realize how muddy the pond's going to become shortly.

"I then commenced to struggle as a Black man setting up something to work. However, it had not always worked the way I wanted it to be. If another White man or even my own Black men wanted it for themselves, both parties, when given the chance, would continue to push it outta business until its dead. However, the White man is the worse. If he couldn't get it for himself, he would prefer to push some other White men in authority to wipe it out clean."

Chapter Seventeen

"Then the White man would bawl like a pregnant woman giving birth; the Black men shouldn't get this and shouldn't get that. It was screwy, very screwy, and it simmered down to one point: trust no other bastard except one's mother. That's because she carried you and never strangled or aborted you when you were a baby. I learned that the hard way; anything beyond motherly trust, I forget about. Besides, I didn't have one anymore. I trust God and no two-footed bastard would ever earn that privilege again. Nothing was strange to us all along. They would use the taxman, the council, and their buddies to bring our business to its knees."

BRANDON (*pondering*)
Maybe it's because we're not complying with this and that. But suppose Borer retires....

"They might hold it by the neck and strangle it until the business was no more. Then we won't see the bastard again; that was how it had been all the time. Shank and I discussed this dreaded portion. More than a few times, it came up that it might make our office and business to really go down the pan. Without Borer around to tittle the system, we might as well hang up before he does goes.

"He could blow our cover anytime. Since the taxpayers didn't know why I had snatched the money from a cop's fund, it would be of less concern to them whether I would be sent down for twenty odd years or for life. It remained hard for them to understand. I had been working for different firms of accountancy up until I realized that, as I was coming up for promotion, I would be fired. This trend was repeated until I was already not so sure what the next issue to be aroused would be, knowing it would not be long or far away before another issue arose as detrimental as before or even worst would come.

"So I set up my own little investment company, seeing that insurance and investment bond was mainly for the higher society and those opulent sorts. It paid the bills from the commissions and left a few pounds to spare after the monthly payment on the Merck coupe. It was then when I looked at the equilibrium of labour. That's when I asked my aunt whether her son, Fritz Bouncy, would join the outfit. My aunt was a tall and slim woman. She was kind to us, her sister's children, and a Sunday churchgoer. She would call for us or telephone if I would like to come to church functions with her. Mother would always start to prepare us from Friday after school.

"On Saturday, there were columns of reminders by Mother that I would be going with my aunt to church. Sometimes, the sermon never seemed to stop. An hour or more in a child's life listening to something he can't understand is a long time. I never did understand why Mother wouldn't go to church. When Aunt came to pick me up, Fritz would be smartly dressed, spread out on the back leather seat of the Oxford super saloon; he was dressed up like a penguin.

"He was in the choir and went off to some places I hardly heard about. When he returned, he adapted this greater-than-thou unspeakable arrogance. I could not tell what rightly happened, but Aunt remained squeaky whenever Fritz's father was mentioned by name. I supposed it was caused by his father running off with a seventeen-year-old from the kitchen hand."

AUNT
Fingers stink; you can't cut it off, Brandon. That's very honourable of you. Like real family should be.

BRANDON
Glad to help out when I can, Aunt.

AUNT
He still misses his father; it causes him to upset the family so much.

BRANDON
Aunt I'm just giving him a job. If he plays faces, then he'll be out as quick as he comes in. And it might well be that way out.

AUNT
Blood's thicker than water, Mow matter what others may advice and say.

"Aunt Bouncy said farewell and hang up. I hadn't seen Fritz. It was going some three years since I spoke to him; most of the time, I avoided him. But he was family.

"He came to my certification passes out at our local university. I had glimpsed him with one of my former girlfriends sometime after. He looked me in the eye and told me he wasn't screwing her.

"Then, a week later, when I had gone through the pain, the woman came and said she was sorry, confirming the truth. They had been going out behind my back for two months while I was seeing another girl, Pesto Henson—a good thing I wasn't duped by having one woman, else I could have easily ended up with none."

BRANDON

How would you like to join Willows Associate? Pay's good and with incentive. If you proved to be any good, you'll get more.

FRITZ

Okay, Bran. When's start?

"Fritz got a sort of articulated, magniloquent streak. He was like a con artist and was one. He sometimes practiced the depth of his abilities to entice others to believe in his power."

BRANDON

Say, a week or so?

"I replied, knowing before the day was out, he'd be around seeking loans or something else. It was a week later when Fritz joined the outfit Willows Accountancy. Within few weeks of his engagements, Fritz was pulling in the clients and doubling our intake and my prosperity; WA could employ a part time clerk who looked after filing letters and general office needs. Fritz was rewarded handsomely for his part. However, he worked Annette Hand, our clerk, so much that the girl almost cried out.

"I presumed the blond sometime left the office talking to herself, saying she wouldn't turn up for work the next day. But Fritz had a hold on her. He duped her to believe she would be the next in line for promotion, and somehow, she managed to turn up, believing his lie. Shortly, when Fritz was promoted to manager, I started to hear rumours about his adopted lifestyle. I couldn't tell what it was about a person when my suspicion started—it just did. If the suspect would approach this matter, he would strongly deny any wrongdoing."

BRANDON

Hear that you're screwing some of the clients, not that they're like a woman, but their money. Give me some leaning, Fritz. Tell me what I'm hearing isn't so.

FRITZ

Think I could do that to WPIA? Man, don't let me cry. How could I do that to WPIA when it gives me such a break? Trusted me to be a manager and all the other things it gives me. No, Bran, couldn't do it, old chap.

"He was sad and seemed sincere."

FRITZ

Only White men can do that, but I'm one of you—us! You're my own blood and flesh, travelling on the same planet that demonizes us from creation because of our colour.

Chapter Eighteen

BRANDON

Tell me the old, old story of Fritz and his love! If this song wasn't written for a good man, then you would 'a fit the opposite perfectly.

"WPIA was making good money. I could spend a little more on showing the prosperity side, but I was keeping my ears to the ground. Fritz was known to have two diaries: one for private use and the other for WA appointments. I gave him a long list of purchasers from various organisations. He was to mark all contacts from the file after he had established contact with them. However, purchasers would not be contacted twice about the same issue.

"Tabasco Wall unexpectedly visited the office one midday. I had done some business for him some time ago. He was one of those White men who one hated to have their trust because they trust you implicitly. There, investments of an honest man he guarded with his own life. However, Tabasco Wall had money to the ends of the earth and invested in anything going. That's why I supposed he got so much money. He liked to take risks and sometimes won big rewards. He acted like a consultant to firms, saying when they should or should not move into location where money from the government would be flowing.

"I doubted very much if he hadn't got something on WPIA's life span, style, or duration at some other investment house. He had some bets on a banking house whose turnover was a bit too small for that year. Soon, the banks would be in trouble. Some city slickers put up something against him, and they lost, hands down.

"That time when Tabasco walked into WPIA's office, he walked in bigger than he was large. He wouldn't let Annette Hand take his coat by herself to the hanger unless I told her to do so. He wore a wide-pleated suites and chequered cap—that of the handicap sort. His loafer was a little bit tight, and I thought his feet were swollen, but he had managed uncomfortably wearing them.

"Fritz would be coming in late that day, if at all. I called for Tabasco Wall's files from Mow, knowing I had safely guarded his identity as requested. I used numbers to identify a client's name. Nothing was so strange when I used the Wingding symbols the computer processor provided adequately.

"The policeman's benevolent investment fund documents were filed under the same headings. These included taxpayers' money, part of their income, and Bobbie's contributions to their own dangerous undertakings. I had no doubt that the papers at the WPIA office and their investment was with a good suitor. Besides that, I kept the full transactions in written work order, which was user-friendly.

"Tabasco Wall sat in the suite as though he was going to bust, not with rage, I was sure, but from overindulgence in his lifestyle. He always seemed to be in a hurry to finish everything, even so to a hot mug of coffee; he put it away in seconds while I frantically searched for his written document. Mr. Wall was a big White man; I was a midget at five eleven and a half. He was about right when he sat on the suite uncomfortably; he opened his crutch so wide that it spread and filled the two seats fully."

TABASCO
> Mr. Willows, I'm going to do something across the road. I'll see you shortly; back in a tick.

BRANDON
> I'm sure when you come back, we'll have everything ready for you to sign up and we'll be on our way, Mr. Wall.

"He had just turned through the swinging doors. I watched him went to the lift, waiting for a little while. Then he entered the lift and was gone. Annette, I knew, suspected that the files had gone missing. I observed that she was uncomfortable when my search went wandering."

BRANDON
> You shouldn't have seen those files, but I'll ask you. Did you see them?

"She replied curtly."

MOW
> Not myself, but I saw Mr. Bouncy looking at some papers. Maybe it's them. Maybe it's not. I don't know.

"She shrugged her shoulder."

BRANDON
> Are you sure? What sort of paper?

MOW

Well, let's say he went into the filing system there and took out some papers. Then he sat sifting through them. I pretended I wasn't looking. Then he put them into his briefcase. That's all.

"I knew that if Fritz knew what he was doing, then he could wipe out WA. A short time following Tabasco Wall's leave and Annette's confirmation, there were feelings of being dead or me wanting it to happen right there and then. I got no recollection of the time because time wasn't important anymore.

"Time had gone by and left my space empty. Suddenly, four government men entered the office. They were fraud and security officers from Inland Revenue. They wanted all the papers and transaction from five years or more of our trading standard procedures. Not even the pencil could I move. If I was seen blinking, they would have a surgeon pulling out my eyeballs for hidden documents, too."

GOVERNMENT MAN

You shouldn't have done it, Mr. Willows. I had advised you not to do anything foolish. Right now, we're confiscating all your business affairs.

ANNETTE

Mr. Willows didn't do anything; Mr. Bouncy did it. He did it.

BRANDON

Talk to that man over there; he must be the head.

GOVERNMENT MAN

We can't do anything for you, Mr. Willows. He's a bad guy. Have anything to say? We will enlighten you on these matters.

"I clapped my hands together and went to find out who had been complaining to the IRS (Internal Revenue Service) to zip us up."

DON SQUISHY

You're going to tell me that you know nothing about it, aren't you, Mr. Willows?

BRANDON

Damn right as well. Let's say I'm in the dark. I run a good outfit here. Making a few bucks here and there. I am just trying to earn a living. Then you came along, wanting to destroy it.

"Don Squishy didn't care much about my concern. He closed the place and was now going through the filing cabinets, he and his wolves. He slowed the rampaging a little, rested his elbow on top of the filing cabinet, and made a swing."

DON SQUISHY

We would strongly advise you, Mr. Willows, not to try and leave the country before this investigation's complete.

Chapter Nineteen

BRANDON
How long that'll be?

"Another of the government men stepped in."

GOVERNMENT MAN
Long as it takes.

"Shank leaned against the door."
SHANK
That'll wipe us out?

GOVERNMENT MAN
Not our concern, Mrs. Willows. Have a job to rap you blokes up; that's what I'm doing. Fall outta line and we send you and your likes down. Got it?

"I was considering a fight, but two other of the gorillas stood abreast when he returned to what he was doing. Meanwhile, Tabasco Wall came through the door. At first, I thought it was he who had complained, but he was as much surprised at what he had seen. He asked me what was going on; I didn't answer him because I didn't know what was going on myself."

BRANDON
Ask the boss man there.

"I watched Tabasco walk away, across to where Squishy was standing with his back turned toward us. I didn't move at all except for the general human scratch here and there and natural parts' movements like eyelids ups and downs as well as movements of the heart and mind, one palpitating while the other travelling along the prison cell that was to come later. Tabasco Wall was carrying on as though he had owned WPIA. If anyone could get WPIA off the hooks, then it would be Tabasco. He got money—and big. He had asked whether I had found his files."

MOW

I was looking for them when these bloodhounds arrive shortly after you leave. Sorry, Mr. Wall, but you can't have any of your documents. Our search was stopped by them, those two. Fritz could cause problems. He's going to bring some new customer. He told me that two of those would boost the cash flow to our office.

SHANK

Why would that be? Clean, aren't you?

BRANDON

They won't identify anything because your name's coded.

TABASCO

These bastards will; I know them.

"Tabasco whispered so loud that those men must have heard him. Nonetheless, they didn't show any concern."

TABASCO

You, though, will need a priest.

BRANDON

What for? I did nothing wrong.

TABASCO

You'll need one for when they bury you on consecrated ground.

"He waved his index."

TABASCO

Mark my word.

"Then the big man walked through the swing door and was gone. Fritz didn't turn up for the day. I telephoned my aunt, leaving several messages for him to get in touch ASAP; I need to tell that the feds' boys we're out and the place was locked up. If he had gotten there, then he would have seen the signs 'Closed until further notice' on the top windows and on the entrance.

"My private account was locked away at the bank. Annette Hand's personal cheque bounces another mile on the company's account. Everything stopped; my life, too. The Merck coupe was gone. Aunt Maud rang me later that evening; I told her not to say anything over the line."

BRANDON
Maybe bugged by the listening authorities.

AUNT
I have an idea what's happening to you, Brandon. I think it's Fritz. Sorry.

"She confirmed my thought regrettably."

BRANDON
Have any ideas where I might find him, Aunt?

MAUD
I would try the police station.

BRANDON
What he's doing there?

MAUD
They picked him up trying to sell some papers.

BRANDON
Of course. I should have guessed. Thanks, Aunt.

"I didn't want to go any further talking to my aunt. Fritz knew of my private stock, and he would sell his mother if the cops give him a sweet; he didn't care.
"I knew well of Fritz's standard—being untrustworthy—and when it boiled down to his pound of steak, he wanted it all. I climbed over both heads and arranged to see Steve at the prison by covert vocabulary method. Partial break came when I decided to lean on Steve a little bit more than I would if it had been on another time and event. Besides, he was now in remand for a few weeks, without any judiciary decision to prison or not to prison him."

STEVE
I now have nothing to say to you. When I help you and you gone with your big job and I left here to rot. I did tell you dot, mess about with dem, and dem will see you hang first. I hear more tings in here that going to bus up your head, but me nah tell you dem.

BRANDON
Well, buddy, if that's the way you feel, dem a gone dweth. I'm closer to you, man. So look, Steve, help me out and I'll see what I can do. You

heard that I'm a good man. You must've also heard that I have some schooling here, too, as a bad man.

STEVE
Den what you're saying?

"He looked at me shrewdly and smiled."

STEVE
Den, Mr. Willows—me earn knows dot, you cum a dis yaw place, too?

BRANDON
Yes, I was a student here.

"I remarked that I might have to join by choice the higher learning again for info."

Chapter Twenty

STEVE

That is something. Welcome mek; we talk no.

BRANDON

Yes, that's what I'm here for, Steve.

"Meantime, at the review meetings, the management was considering the news report regarding the merger, which was also obliging for anyone with information to send it along. I had written to the office and asked to be self-represented at the hearing. I then asked DuPont to strengthen my case by sort of tying up a few legal fluffs that may spuriously come away from the garment and to stop or reduce the impact of the evidences I had obtained. Shortly after, I went at the PD to see Borer, knowing he might have something himself to say. However, I didn't get anything since he voiced in Shank's presence that he had thought we were tailing off the investigation to his liking."

BORER

So tell me, Willows, what have you been up to lately? Know that you visit Steve in prison. Have you got anything to report from your observation?

BRANDON

I visit the poor sod only as an acquaintance. Can't leave the guy there to rot; his wife nor his mother won't go to see him, not yet, while some of his family won't go near the place. They're afraid they may be implicated in his wrongs, so they won't go to see him even if they haven't committed any crime. Just fearing.

BORER

I think I did warn you to keep away from Steve?

BRANDON
>Course. To tell you the truth, the World Aircraft Associates has given us the creeps. Had I been looking for something as fault-finding or something we could see or know something about like what if these had taken place in the real world, I might have encounter serious problems. What would happen then?

"He slapped his hands on the table, showing his annoyance with me."

BORER
>You're new to this field, Willows, and Shank. Consider your child first and foremost. Better to have a little jam on your toast than none at all.

BRANDON
>Why is it that I smell a threat in your statement? I will be requesting a favour from you shortly, Sir. The pay is good—they paid well for doing almost nothing; that, I don't like. I like to earn my keeps.

BORER
>Okay, when you're ready. I'm always happy to oblige someone.

"His voice dropped into a drably growled."

BORER
>While you're not going to take advantage or something outside the law, keep the nastiness out of it, if you can, Willows. That man, Steve, will be your downfall.

BRANDON
>I can't—working in the mire already. Everybody expects to smell a bit of perfume when working in that area where shits are, so as those acquainted with the sewer.

"I left the PD that afternoon and went home to see Shank. Fritz left a message on the answering machine to meet him at the Dragon ASAP. The Dragon was where we have had our first shot of whisky, and we never forget to stop off there when something newsy is in the offing. We moved up rank since, but now, our liquor was reduced to lemonade, water, or orange soda and zilch in on anything stronger for the road. Fritz came in the office that afternoon to give some rundown about WAA, but things were going the other way which none of us liked very much. It was dangerous waters. We concluded that the WPIA was treading the mill like a mouse on a treadmill."

FRITZ
>Ah, Savaggy held another party last weekend.

"He twisted the glaze with its clear water, twirling around and looking on as though he was a reader of the future."

BRANDON

What they're celebrating this time? Know who were there?

"He popped out of his inner coat pocket a list of names. Some of the names were in the circular hearsay while others were meaningless. Shank, who have more learning skills, sat down, she and Mow, to work around and solve some of the names Fritz pulled."

FRITZ

Some of those names are familiar. What you say, Bran, 'bout Mow and me, you know?

BRANDON

Not now, Fritz; you're getting warm. Taking on the woman from our office. Tell Borer? Know what that means, don't you?

"He had a smile while he pulled at his warty beard."

BRANDON

Should I... and Shank, too?

FRITZ

Swear, Bran, shouldn't give you any trouble.

"Meanwhile, I'd briefly discussed Mow and Fritz getting together. It was midnight when Shank had woken me to tell met she was glad. I wasn't sure about Fritz's ability; I reserved my judgement for later. The next morning, I'd a chance to run up the names and compare with the list Fritz had obtain on the computer. How he'd come by it didn't matter. Later...

"A few names were familiar; we already know about there. However, there was one name that commenced to rings bells in my ear. I screened, in my mind, for the name. It bogged my operational screw with corrosion since there was no face to it. It was a hunch I could not drop for a second of the day.

"At the first WAA hearing, the case presented was why the aircraft should not merge with a worldwide consortium and remain in BAID control. It wasn't long after when correspondence from unknown firms started to arrive on the WPIA office, which then opened the floodgates to uncover who we were, making us doubtful of whether there were some bastards subjecting us to their investigation. Albeit, the ponds were becoming exceptionally muddy."

Shank telephones DuPont.

DuPont

Mrs. Willows, we cannot tell you anymore of the WAA's decision or when we will be meeting again, not unless you pull some strings from the top of your end. I am obviously doubtful if it is possible in this case.

Shank

Why is he doing this to us? Trouble on line one.

DuPont

Of course, I could send out some papers, mistakenly marked "Top secret." No trouble if it comes to your address, read it, and send it back. Savvy?

"Angle on the insider playing gulf at his local club: Massey was with another who plays with him. They arrived a little earlier and were well-known to Savaggy. Maybe it was coincidental, but he was playing and mulling in with shattered laughter. Fritz was taking the picture of the players during the late summer evening, positioning near the golf course.

"It was at home in the afternoon two weeks later that Fritz and Mow came to have a bite. Fritz popped out some photographs with some shots capturing Mow and another face in the background. It was particularly interesting."

Mow

Careful! Looking as though you're about to fall in love with the picture, Bran.

Brandon

Who's the face in the background?

Chapter Twenty-One

FRITZ

It may have been a scattered shot, never meant to. That person showed up, but we can't tell how the camera pulled it in so close. Why? Somebody you know?

"I didn't answer; I contacted Borer at once."

BRANDON

I got a name and a picture. I'll fax it to you, the picture.

BORER

No, don't do that; meet me. Bring Mow along. Clever surveillance now—enables the redirection of these sorts of things.

"Shank had shown she wanted to come along as much. I agreed. Fritz and Mow were not at the WAA hearing a month later. Shank went to her normal monthly check-up after the meeting, and I went with her. I could smell a man and woman as they walked towards us, sitting in a waiting department of the clinic."

WOMAN

Mrs. Willows?

SHANK

Why? Yes, I am Mrs. Willows.

WOMAN

We are here to arrest you for not attending your court hearing.

SHANK

When was that? I...I thought that was finished. I was promised that we wouldn't be summoned over the misinterpretation.

"I moved across to the man standing as though on frightened ground, or the other way around."

BRANDON

This is a pregnant woman you're starting to harass.

MAN

Sorry, Sir. We have to take her in, arrest her. Got a job to do for gov'. We'll wait until the doctor attend to her. By then, you'll have time to arrange something for her to be home tonight. I know how you feel, Sir, got a little boy myself.

BRANDON

How about if you leave her with me, and we'll come along in the morning to make her apologize to the court? Know a couple of bailiffs who'd grant that?

MAN

See what can be done.

"We moved over to Shank where they were talking woman stuff."

SHANK

We'll go back to the office. Promise me, Mrs. Willows, that you'll come up the court tomorrow morning for the.... I'll arrange for you to see a judge quickly.

"He then wrote on a bailiff's pad the time when he would be attending the court next morning. I asked Borer to let me take some statement from Steve as he was part of the filing system. Steve got into the crowd where carpet layers were as thick as an old barn house design, under cover and over. He was employed at BAID in low a class work, not of his choice but of the system placing him there. Steve was put in charge of shifting papers at the place for filing. He noticed the name I'd shown to him and recognized him. He said it was a guy named Sawyers. Sawyers had been registered dead for some time from the firm, but his name continued to crop up on the filing system, with pay cheque as though he was alive, well, and able."

STEVE

Come along there sometime. But not often. Make me see....

"He paused and continued for a minute or so."

STEVE

A think...his name crops up a few times, well, around de place when I was filing away some de documents. He is de hit man for BAID, I hear. He kills people, su you watch you and him.

"Meanwhile, a long lens binocular panned BAID's gate from a woodland overlooking the firm's entrance. It was afternoon. Along drove a grey-coloured Jaguar-type saloon. It went through the gate and stopped. A character came out of the car, but it was not the driver. He walked up to the door and through the reception."

BRANDON

Could be anybody. But that walks seems familiar.

"She was going to say something rather shocking, it seemed. She paused and dug a knifepoint into the bread I bought for lunch."

SHANK

Think he'll shit on you again, Bran?

BRANDON

Suspect Fritz, am I not right, honey? Entirely a matter of the guy being some big, selfish be....

SHANK

Don't swear. I know he's a shit house brick. Exactly! What? He makes us a few bobs, though.

BRANDON

Your father must've hated what you love, honey. Desperate man.

"I then knew from the convincing evidence compiled that we weren't able to keep things under wraps any longer. It's a matter of who would get hurt and who would be hurting both of us deeply. At the MMMC enquiry two days later, the prisoner came in and was pining against two HMPS officers. Later....

"Just before the hearing, I made my way to a row behind where Borer was with his colleagues. Mow was not invited at the hearing, but Fritz was summoned to appear as part of the key witnesses. They were late coming in with Steve."

BRANDON

Sure he will be here in time, DIB?

BORER

Be, patient, Brandon.

"Shortly, while the hearing progressed, two persons from HMPS came through the heavy-gauge door. Steve was in the middle and handcuffed to both. He was our key witness whose evidence the Crown Court sorted almost at once."

STEVE

Sawyers has been dead for some time now.

"He pointed to Fritz."

STEVE

That is de man I always know as Sawyer. But that one there.

"He pointed at Massy."

STEVE

And that one there.

"He pointed at Savaggy."

STEVE

Bad man dem. Is real sleaze bags dem is.

BORER

The old proverb can never be wrong, Willows. Don't put all your eggs in one basket.

BRANDON

Yeah. I'll remember that for a long time.

"He leaned across on the shiny courtroom seats and whispered."

BORER

Just who is your friend? The one who dips his hands in the bowl with me? Isn't that so, Willows?

Chapter Twenty-Two

BRANDON
Not mine. Those two bastards. Fritz's behaviours can never be controlled. Don't know how my aunt came to bear such b....

"I whispered loudly, unconcerned of who would hear me."

BORER
All right, Willows, I get your point.

"Another two mouths burden for the taxpayers to feed: that's nothing big. When I closed my book, Borer was still holding out that I would be one of the good guys. I most certainly commended him for having such staunch faith in my ability because Shank became his adopted daughter though he was not so sure about me.

"When Shank got our baby, she promised that if things worked out well, she would be going onto the matrimonial side of things because it's a buzzing industry. For a while, with the likes of Fritz, babies, and my henchman, I could now boast that I got the geniality to father a child.

"Meantime, I reasoned out and considered that there may be reason why they did not have enough revulsion to sell out the whole of WAA to even Tabasco so they would have benefited themselves and their insatiable appetite for the higher-ups and just walk away with millions in their pockets, letting the taxpayers pick up the prevention of the aircraft from falling into the likes of the Al-Qaeda. Only then could they still pull their puppet strings although away from the action zones.

"Steve's case came up for hearing. He was given bail by the court for being lenient, following some argument by DuPont, and of his previous good behaviour. What happened to the crow that was following him around? It disappeared. Massey's son was released, too. Shank and I asked both Fritz and Massey's son to join WPIA on lower schemes when they were finally released;

it was to be considered. By the way, I was still waiting for Shank. We might have our baby earlier since she had been having quite a lot of trouble carrying her little son. We had a wedding to attend down the West Indies sometime in the future.

"Fritz was a man who had grown out of envy for the family. That son of a bitch strived on making the rest of us uncomfortable when he's around. He was spiteful as an enemy and cut throat as a friend. Nobody could doubt his sincerity, lying along these lines.

"I had gone that afternoon to visit the car rental company. It wasn't far, about fifty miles through the city centre going south, which took about two and a half hours while negating several obstacles going through like traffic lights, slowness, and all that diversion preventing me to get where I was going on time. The early evening news said that a man had tried to dive off one of the high riser en route to the direction I was travelling.

"A number of sirens from varying departments were screeching: fire, police, and the ambulances. I could see Constable Pan Ray from the local station controlling the traffic. He was youngish and had served in the Gulf when Iraq and the Allied countries conflict. These guys seldom have any hang-ups about natural selection and as I didn't have any, we get on just fine."

PAN
  Hi, Mr. Willows.

"Pan was walking toward my vehicle and I had fully wound the windows down."

BRANDON
  Hi, Pan. What's going on?

PAN
  Guys up there want to do a flier.

BRANDON
  And you're trying to stop him from doing so?

PAN
  Part of our job, Mr. Willows.

BRANDON
  Ever consider the Wrights brothers? They were successful doing it.

"I laughed, and he did also."

SHANK

He won't be able to let you stop here, but we can go and find a parking spot then come back that way if you want to do so.

PAN

Yeah, but I haven't got any time. Why don't you pop round sometimes? Got a favour to ask of you.

BRANDON

Sound serious.

PAN

It is. Going to see somebody now. I may have to get the law involved after this.

BRANDON

Glad to help out. Does this involve a guy named Steve?

"I spun the vehicle round and headed out of the city, still going south—southeast. There were several parking spots available when I got to my destination. I took the one nearest to the entrance and shoved the small vehicle in. The afternoon sun was shining but did not have much heat after the heavy clouds filtered it through. The resulting appearance was reasonable.

"The place had a few executive chairs jacked up against the walls with egg yolk colour. There were two small glass tables, round and square, with two, two-seater chairs each and a few magazines of new-type motors available and various signs of the trade on top.

"The dull grey carpet in the hallway seemed to need changing or steaming to remove the chewing gum spots here and there. Some palm trees had been put into pots near the large glass windows. I rang the bell and stood at the counter, looking around."

WOMAN

Can I help you?

"I didn't look around immediately. I was disappointed. It was a woman's voice, calm and sweet. The fact that, as I stated, I was starving for sexual interaction made any voice of a woman sweet. I had mentioned to Constable Pan that I may see her soon because I had had it in mind wrenching Slouch's head off. Somebody was messing me about, and I didn't know who. Slouch would have to tell who's messing with me. If it is the WAA on undercover investigation, I was hoping to resolve it by buying a camouflage from the WPIA or some other bastards who seemed itching their ride, too. However, it wasn't going to work out very well."

BRANDON
I am sure you can. I am Brandon. Come to see Mr. Slouch.

SLOUCH
Slouch? Back in a minute.

"She went through a swinging door, and for a while, I heard no sound. Then she came back smiling. She had a pleasant smile."

WOMAN
Mr. Slouch will be with you in a few minutes. He's dealing with a customer. Then he'll come straight out to you. Mr. Willows, can I get you something to drink?

BRANDON
No, just had one before I left my place. But if you're going to have one, then I will have one with you.

SHANK
I'll have one with you.

"She said it reassuringly. It seemed that I was eyeing the woman too much while in my wife's presence."

What's your name?

COLET
Colet.

SHANK
Oh!

"She was looking up and down on the front of her dress."

Sorry, I left it down before lunch and I forgot to put it back on. Colet Jamie.

BRANDON
Colet? That's a nice name. Working here long?

COLET
A couple of years, yeah. Just gone two years.

"I knew in my mind that I had started the conversation to ask her if she had a boyfriend or was married as well as how many children she got, how old she was, and where she was born. All those I wanted to ask her and more as she turned her back to get the water for the coffee from the dispenser while I gazed at her unwillingly, knowing Shank had me weighed up all along, which was a pity, I reasoned."

Chapter Twenty-Three

"I thought I could get in there if there was no immediate obstacle. Nobody sets out to find money, but if somebody saw it available, he or she would pick it up and spend it delightfully. That was supposed to be my hook-up. But Slouch had been forward coming."

BRANDON
   Pay's good?

COLET
   Not bad.

   "She was walking back to the cups that had been laid out on her side of the counter."

POLICEMAN
   You were here when the Mr. Willows booked the vehicle?

COLET
   No, I wasn't. My little boy got the chicks, and I had to stay at home with him. Quarantined myself for a whole week. But Bryan will be with you in the next few minutes, Mr. Willows.

BRANDON
   Is he your brother?

COLET
   I don't have any brother. A couple of sister doesn't bother much with me. One's in Canada and the other in the States. Got some rich blokes looking after them.

"Colet was with slightly bronze skin and black jet hair. She had worn it long and shaggy. I wasn't sure if her eyes were blue or she had been wearing makeup that was reflected by her eyeballs. She might be about a hundred and thirteen pounds and stood around five- five. From both parents, she was of natural selection, and like Shank, just a bit larger around the hips. A bloke who must have heard us talking came along and peeped. He didn't stop long, though, but he causally went away.

"I was sipping some coffee slowly, hoping to prolong my discussion with Colet, when I had noticed a security camera peeping at me. I could not tell whether it was loaded, but it was focusing at me. It seemed as though it was not a static setup above the counter overlooking the yard. I had divulged that it made it sweep and take in the whole of the frontage."

BRANDON
Mr. Slouch seems to be taking his time.

"I turned to her. By then, two men of the security type had walked into the building. But they didn't come directly to the counter where Colet and I were conversing; they were timely moving about, pretending to read the older office magazines. I was thinking by then whether they were being dumb or blind. I was in the security business and know quite well when people came for something. And that something could be me."

BRANDON
Know them?

"I had to ask Colet. Massey and Borer had warned me that I should back off from Steve's case, and both men weren't men, it seemed, to be messed with. Bulldozer, Massey's son, was in the slammers, and it was only Steve who could shag it outta him. Bulldozer's mother could have put pressure from within for him to be released. If that was the case, then Massey could be speeding up the pressure on Steve to get the information before Bulldozer was released for whatever reason he was imprisoned for. Slouch was surveying who were in his office before he came out to see me or meet the others who were there."

COLET
Sometimes, people just wander off the street to see what is in here.

BRANDON
No, Colet. These are not wanderers. These are the genuine stuff. They are coppers. Owed any VAT? Know of any serious things going on around here?

"I could almost see the eyes peering through the camera lenses."

MAN

This is an upfront establishment, Mr. Willows; it is going for over fifty years. We supply quality vehicles to the hiring public and industry. Never have any problems, as far as I understand, in its fifty-year history.

BRANDON

Let's get back to your son. Is he all right now?

COLET

Oh, yes. He's back at school over a month.

BRANDON

Is he your only child?

COLET

Mr. Willows, one's enough. Thank you. Can't afford to have anymore.

BRANDON

Supposed your husband wants a girl or something?

COLET

I'm not married, Mr. Willows. I am just a plain and simple mum.

BRANDON

You're kidding?

WOMAN

That's right. I am just a plain and simple mother.

"Colet put her elbows and leant forward on the counter. For over five minutes, the two suspected cops were moving about, gazing out on the frontage, pretending and flipping through the magazines. One of them was about thirty-five years old and about 5'11". His attire was a black suit with some stripes going vertical from the classic assortment of the bailiff's sorts.

"The other was slightly smaller with bulging guts and must have, sometime or the other, suffered from overindulgence. His eyes were popping out of his little head; weighing him up, he should be the one in charge. That guy never knew what was in a twenty-four-hour day. At the same time, I was sure he tried to have twenty-six hours a day to make up his pay cheque as aggrieved bonuses."

BRANDON

'Bout time you see what they want.

COLET

I'm employed to service the counter and already pressed for someone to come out.

"I surmised that Colet wasn't strictly truthful at that point. I had some idea she was willing to cover up something. And might it be that Bryan was into something bigger. Damn! If someone came along to see WPIA about the urgent problems as I had extrapolated over the telephone, I would not have to see them at once. Particularly, we were trying to solve the problems of the vehicle and besides that, someone who was trying to mar my name.

"It was a why Mr. Slouch was impolite and downright rude, and although I admired Colet's femininity, I had resorted to ripping her head off as well. It was a stitch up even had he was on calls from across the sea.

"Colet had now gone back through the door. I noticed that she was swinging her hips as she went. The sequence of past events dwelled on my mind for about a minute when she returned. She must have suspected that I had sussed out that things weren't normal by now. Her facial expression wasn't pleasant anymore, and I didn't want to ask why."

BRANDON

Mr. Slouch has two minutes more to take my call, and I'll be seeing him after that.

"I then set my Seiko watch to buzz when two minutes had passed."

BRANDON

Plenty of time to give to another business without doing actual business.

"I knew he was listening through the surveillance camera. It had just turned fifty-two second when an elderly, half-bald White man appeared almost from nowhere through the swing door. He pushed his hands forward for the usual courtesy."

BRANDON

I believe in the natural selection method, Mr. Slouch. I think you're rude. That's over fifteen minutes that you kept me waiting.

"He apologized, but it was not truthfully accepted, but I didn't have the time to prolong the why and wherefores."

BRANDON

Let's get down to the problems I'm having this morning. Just before your call, there was another telling us that I had stopped off in Wales Hotel and Resort for a week. Then you came and stated that I hired your motor for a month?

SLOUCH
Mister...?

BRANDON
Brandon.

SLOUCH
Well, Mr. Willows. Let me outline our business. We've been in the vehicle hiring business for over fifty years, and we trust that we run a good business. Why? Because our customers always return. That's our measuring stick.

"When our conversation started, the two goons moved forward. Slouch was now dealing with me, and he was going to stay there until I got the information I came for."

BRANDON
Could you tell me how the vehicle was hired from here, Mr. Slouch?

Chapter Twenty-Four

SLOUCH (*at a hotel*)

We have a policy here which has been going about two decades now. Someone wants to hire a vehicle, they rang us up. We ask for their company name and details, their account number and address. We run a quick check, and we ask the person or the firm to pick up the vehicle from our main depot. If they can't pick it up themselves, we drop the vehicle off where they designate. When the vehicle returns, we calculate the amount and the firm pays us whether in cheque or direct debit. However, direct debit is the usual route most people take. I trust that you will bring back our car, Mr. Willows, and you have found it satisfactory.

BRANDON

What sort of car was it?

SLOUCH

Top of BM range; was a good choice; I have one of them. I like the ride. Trust that you have enjoyed the style and the beautiful finish. See on your file; you were the first to drive this one.

BRANDON

Mr. Slouch, I know nothing about this hiring of your vehicle, and there's no way I could change my colour. Feel me; I am the real thing. See?

"I was becoming riled, and my heart was doubling up in, constantly bursting out. I flew a button on my shirt, pushed my hand through the hole, tried to hold onto my heart. I could have done so with a large something to calm the damn pumping down."

SLOUCH

As a matter of a fact, Mr. Willows, we received a call from somewhere in Derbyshire. They are saying that our vehicle has been parked on their hotel park for over a week ago, and they have found a WPIA business card left in their hotel and in our vehicle. So, they asked us to confirm your details. We did, of course. That was after I had spoken to you.

"The bald man's face dropped when he continued."

SLOUCH

Course, that car was in an accident, and from what I can gather, it is writhing off. Come to think of it, it wouldn't be able to return to our fleet even if they do get it fixed.

"Fritz came into the office the day before and told us that he and Mow were hoping to get a weekend together. I couldn't say much about Fritz or Mow's plans because Shank was all along the line of giving Fritz the benefit of the doubt; she was treating him like a brother which I hadn't come to expect. Knowing Fritz's make up, I was sort of scared when he comes around and I had to be leaving him alone with Shank.

"Bryan called as I wandered away from the matter at hand. I was reasoning on Mow and Fritz and whether they had been slipping away in the evening after work to some resort hotel; Fritz was capable of doing such chameleon tricks. However, I had reservation about the principle of him doing so. I was thinking aloud."

BRANDON

Hmm...don't know why.

SLOUCH

Why? What is it, Mr. Willows?

BRANDON

Somebody is trying to shag us. But whoever that son of a bitch is who's trying to do us in I'm going to catch up with him and bash his blasted head in. Trying to ruin me.

HOTEL REPRESENTATIVE

Of course, this has taken on far-reaching consequences for your company, you know that?

"Suddenly, I thought about the whole matter and how it could be resolved by the hotel resort: they must have seen the bastard and fed the bastard if he had been there for a week."

HOTEL

Course, we can easily solve it.

"I guessed that Colet was hearing things if she was by the monitor. I would like to get onto her books but couldn't due to this immediate problem. I spent five years away from humans and the female species.

"Prison officers dropped off all human belonging and put on the animal instinct when they came in to work. They wear through the duration of their shifts. Far away HMPS removed us from any indulgence—better if I was on the moon or some other planet. I had seen grown men shag their dick's head off by trying to drill through walls just to have an erection."

GOON

Could I see some papers from you?

BRANDON

What paper would you like to see and what the hell are you talking about?

"They both came out with the incidental badge. The next afternoon, two policemen came to visit. They were both from CID: A. Pepper and R. Rouse."

BRANDON

I could smell you from when you came in, although I wasn't sure which departments. I thought you are from the vat or something else.

"I pulled out my pass, too."

BRANDON

We're working on the same side. Only thing's, you're directly employed; I'm a contractor with the PD. Take up my whole morning and the whole day for that matter.

"Pepper, Rouse, and I walked away from the area to the frontage; Slouch never joined us after then at the resort. I was led to believe that they had someone in mind. Then there was an operation within the organisation but conducted behind the big ideals; the operations were carried out from across the country, making millions of bucks.

"Such an operation behind the big deals friskily told us that they wanted a camouflage to make it seem as though someone was after the secrets regarding the new developments on that twenty-first century aircraft. It would cause the government, whether they like it or not, to push money to prevent it from happening on a wider scale."

BRANDON

This operation is being conducted across the country, making millions of bucks.

PEPPER

We want to nail those shits.

ROUSE

Could we rely on your cooperation, Mr. Willows?

BRANDON

You may have to go through Borer, my boss. Don't touch Whitehall yet.

ROUSE

Who's he?

PEPPER

One of them bright sparks. Thinks he'll be replacing Borer. They never come this far in the east, but we would like to nail them before they get to third target. They always start off being small. If it's not nailed, it will grow.

ROUSE

Everybody in business will have to be warned—people who have their accounts here with you, Mr. Slouch. They normally get about three to four vehicles from each rental company.

BRANDON

Course, we always pay by cheque. Anybody can cream off the cheque number and hand it to some unscrupulous vendor. Could call up the bank and change the account number, if that would help.

"Pepper beckoned Slouch to come over and join as we were sitting in the company of three."

ROUSE

You always traded this way over the telephone?

SLOUCH

Sometimes, we don't even saw our customer or knew who they are. They just order what vehicle they wanted. Sometimes, we have contractors hired to drive our cars to a said destination. What the person or entire firm does is just sign the delivery document. That vehicle will be written off and will be back on the road within days of it being sold, Mr. Pepper.

HALF-BALD MAN
Honestly, it would be hard to stop them with the way we traded without distressing our customers.

"I supposed Colet could not hear what we were saying over her monitor so she had crept back to the service counter. The four men sat at one of the table, speaking slowly and low as though anything heard outside an inch would set the place ablaze."

PEPPER
Know of anybody, anybody that would want to screw you, Mr. Willows?

BRANDON
No one immediately coming to mind. But that Malatya bastard may want to. Could name a dozen without too much thinking. But I don't think they'll go that low. Could be from your gang as well—revenge from your past.

Chapter Twenty-Five

BRANDON
  Been up for, you know.

"I assumed, being an undercover cop, he had to bring out my past in front of strangers. If Slouch picked upon it, he might have understood the colloquial expression 'been up for.' I then commenced to resent the big-eyed bastard because I had no way of knowing what he was thinking when he was trying to hang me out to dry."

BRANDON
  Had nothing to do with what's going on here. You're the employed cops that can't deal with the small timers. So don't you come picking your arseholes around me.

PEPPER
  No harm in asking.

BRANDON
  Pooh! There you had a guy running around with WPIA cards claiming to be me. No Black guy's going to do that and get away with it. You awful sons of a bitch, let me explain again.

ROUSE
  Hmm...hmm. We won't be able to solve the problems without coming together and finding out the connections. We're going do some account exchange.

SLOUCH
  Course, we have several depots.

PEPPER
You take all the bookings from here?

SLOUCH
We do.

PEPPER
So, from here, we may be able to check the son of a bitch.

BRANDON
That's my pitch.

PEPPER
Think Borer will want to hear of this? Borer deals with drugs and related case now—surveillance.

BRANDON
Remember him dealing in frauds and related cases not so long ago?

SLOUCH
I think Whitehall will fall into that slot now.

PEPPER
Good experience to have on board—Borer, I mean.

SLOUCH
Hmm...hmm. Well, gentlemen...

"Slouch yelped, got up from the table, and was ready to go back to work."

SLOUCH
Hope you gentlemen will do something about this mess. Counting on it to happen quickly. Hmm.... About how many vehicles will we be losing with this assistance is not clear as yet?

BRANDON
Not more than four. That's how the trend seems to move.

SLOUCH
The force will pay for all this, will they?

SHANK
We'll see you get cover, Mr. Slouch.

"Shank was showing tiredness when she came in the room and sat on the arm side of the chair (pregnancy-related problem)."

SLOUCH
Fine with me, if that's the case; I'll go along with it. Never dealt with these things before so it is all new to me.

PEPPER
We'll come back to see you again, Mr. Slouch, to straighten out some edges.

SLOUCH
Good.

"Slouch went back to work.
"I had been eyeing Colet. She had frequently been going and coming back to the counter between phone calls. Slouch was too old a White man for her. She needed a bronze man to match her colour. The men and I had agreed to meet urgently with Borer to have his consent so I could continue with the BAID investigation while helping to apprehend a White man going around with my card and bank account number in his pocket.
"I didn't want to say bye to Colet; I just wanted to check her out. Pepper and Rouse walked toward the entrance slowly, unconcerned. I was doing the same when Colet called."

COLET
Mr. Willows. Oh!

"I walked back toward her. She was leaning sideways on the service counter."

COLET
Going without saying goodbye? Course, I been looking in your cup to see what you have up your sleeve.

SHANK
Didn't you see anything down the trousers?

COLET
Didn't go that far, just along the chest and up the brain.

BRANDON
Pooh! What did you want to scan, babe?

COLET
Just what you're thinking. Know I wouldn't do that.

"I know she was lying; it was a trap."

BRANDON
Have lunch with me one day?

COLET
When?

BRANDON
Got a number I could call?

COLET
Yeah. I'll write it for you?

BRANDON
Sure.

At the aircraft silo office.

COLET
Here, you are.

"She wrote her number on a sheet of the company's writing pad and gave it to me. Then I went my way."

BRANDON
Call you 'morrow.

"I folded the sheet in four quarters, stuck it in the breast pocket of my jacket, and slid away. I had hit the evening rush hour at about a third of the journey coming back into the city and didn't encounter any heavy traffic. But then, after the city, I was going NNW. There, I was a delayed a little. At that time, the place where I had passed by the guy trying to fly off a building earlier was clear. Anyway, it was getting late as I remembered I was driving Shank's car.

"Shank had a couple of months to go before the baby comes and didn't want to drive herself. So, she was waiting impatiently for me to get back and take her home. We didn't plan what hit us today. I didn't plan about the hotel resort calling WPIA and the vehicle-hiring place. Neither did I plan to meet Colet. Each problem came with its own problem solving tools.

"Shank wasn't feeling well when we got home, and I had to burn at the stove. I had some stretch rice and a tin of corned beef. It was doused with broad beans mash, ready-made potatoes, and dark-burned scallion to give it some taste. A little over the night, I had a red wine bottle, which Shank did not want to indulge in. I downed the glass and another half of the lot. Shank just wanted to have pineapple juice and more pineapple juice like we were part of the Del Monte family."

BRANDON

I'm sure I could have a quick meal from Mussolini's if I was alone.

SHANK

One minute in women's life they can't cook and there's trouble.

"She said it as if she meant that she was sorry."

BRANDON

Look, dolls. You don't understand what I really meant. Only can cook beans and toast bread.

"I was sorry, too. The child was kicking Shank's guts out."

SHANK

Just hope when he grows up, he'll know what he has done to you.

"She rested her hand on her paunch and laughed."

BRANDON

He sure will. No doubt you're going to tell him about the starvation you underwent.

"I decided not to venture out that evening but I give Borer a telephone call after I got a wash. I enlightened him of what was going on. However, by then, Pepper had already made contact and he was already aware.

"Fritz had been out on surveillance. BAID was paying him directly for his contract work. Borer had decided that I was to help the CID and, while I was doing that, find if there was any drug-related incident that he could lock on as well."

BRANDON

That Pepper guy? Know him some time ago, I supposed.

"I was hoping that Borer would let go of any old grudge."

SHANK

Asked about you and even say he'll probably get you on his team.

BRANDON

That son of a bitch. Well, I'll be darned.

FRITZ

How's Shank?

"Shank was sitting across on a stiff chair for an expectant mother. She had been turned from a beautifully-shaped woman to one in pain and uncomfortable. Her face was dragged. I couldn't believe it, reflecting on my mother carrying me around while my father might have been screwing another woman to satisfy his immediate necessity."

BRANDON

She's okay beside her general problems. Swollen feet and all that stuff.

BORER

Willows? How're you and Shank getting on?

"I couldn't see the man, but the feeling I had gotten was the man on the other end knew something and was asking me."

BORER

Seeing another woman, aren't you?

BRANDON

Why the concern, Borer? Colet is one of us. So my advice is don't fool around. Can't tell you what to do; you are your own man. But I will have to hint Shank about it.

Chapter Twenty-Six

BORER
Okay. What about Fritz and Mow?

BRANDON
None of them related to me.

BORER
Was it Pepper or Rouse?

BRANDON
Both.

BORER
We've got to keep it clean, Willows. We got to keep our self as clean as possible Cops going through a bad patch right now, and everybody's looking in our cupboard.

BRANDON
Okay. Thank you for that advice, DIB. Appreciate it.

"I put the phone back on to its hook and went to sit by Shank. I tried to caress her, rubbing her shoulder and working my hands upward to her tender jaw and over to her lips. Then I moved my hand into her hair and dwell there for a moment. We were like strangers that had seen each other to make love for the first time. I knew that the son of a bitch was still kicking his mother's heart out after, but it was worth it to dose the bugger; I got my way."

SHANK
Everything's okay?

BRANDON

Just another piece of advice from your adopted old copper.

SHANK

He did say what you've just did.

BRANDON

No, darling, just a piece of fatherly advice from a White man. He hopes you'll have a good night rest tonight.

"Shank and I settled down after tea to watch TV. I bought a Harden bedding where she could lie down or sit up when she felt like doing so. We had been living on top of our practice for going nine months. On the upper floor, one of the rooms was larger. That was our living room, decorated in Maria colour and matched for the eye of a woman.

"From the windows, you could see the post office's towers and even to the or-thunder, a Birmingham city landmark. There was a wide open view, and in summer, the view was quite pleasant. From the episode of the day, tiredness had run in my body.

"I just reached the train station with my suitcase to catch the train to visit Steve. He was still in the pen. Fritz came from the opposite platform and boarded the train. He was in authority because he had gotten on the train before it had driven off; I was running behind, yelling."

BRANDON

That is the train I want! That's the train I want!

"Then my suitcase opened, and all the papers flew out. I stopped to retrieve the papers, but the train was gone.

"It was on the morning that Shank had been giggling like her natural self. I knew that having sex was flirty and shouldn't be carried over for the next day unless she wanted more and for me to dose the little bugger again to keep him quiet."

SHANK

Who were you cursing and swearing?

BRANDON

When was that? I thought I was talking about the show then you started to f...ing and going on.

SHANK

I wasn't! You sure were. Telling the person to stop the train.

BRANDON

> Must be Fritz. He wouldn't stop the train to wait for me. And then I had my suitcase which flew open while I was running to catch the train. I stopped to gather up the papers, and by then, the train was gone.

SHANK

> I see. Fritz again, eh? Give the guy a break, man.

BRANDON

> You've given him a full hundred percent. I would hold back, say, five for manoeuvre tolerance, just for probability. Can't say why now. But you should. Nothing's hundred percent pure.

"There were scurrying following the car hiring investigation. Borer asked me to concentrate on the BAID case. However, the following day, DuPont rang and said that he would like to see me at his office to give an update on Steve's case. I had seen Mrs. Boot that same morning. She was in civilian outfit and waved to me.

"I waved back, hoping I would have a word. I went and parked the car, but when I came out onto Soho again, she had gone. I went around a couple corners and peeped into a few of the shops and stores, but I didn't find her.

"Shank got a letter from Savaggy, thanking us for attending his party. She didn't give me the letter to read but I more or less gathered it contained women stuff and probably a few lines of gossip from Mrs. Savaggy. Shank was adequately covering the four pages with a little giggle here and there when I left out to go and see DuPont.

"I then gathered that had Mrs. Savaggy been well-versed with computers or any word processing equipment, she would word process the pages. This I would let Shank be aware of, if she hadn't already guessed and told her to suggest to Mrs. Savaggy, as part of her wasting valuable time, that she could go on part-time course to study modern word processing.

"If she didn't, then it would be no skin off our nose. They could afford what they chose to do on God's land. We were just third party to her husband's chairmanship and his reporting of a saboteur ring going on with his firm. Maybe, just maybe, he wasn't one of the boys from Cambridge or Harrow, Oxford or the sort.

"I was still on my way to see DuPont, travelling SSE, and struggling to come up with what a mess everything had seemed to be. Now, I had wants and needs and wants and needs. Borer wanted to see me at two thirty that afternoon, and I am already running late to see DuPont. I wanted to ring Colet. I wanted to know who was the son of a bitch carrying around my account number and business card."

Chapter Twenty-Seven

"What Fritz and Mow had been up to would be none of our business outside the office, and I wanted to be sure that Shank was all right throughout. However, there were other things I needed to know: why Massey wanted to put Steve in the pen and keep him there, who blew Fritz's place, what happened to Tabasco Wall, where's my freedom, who's my friend, what Jupt was doing down in the West Indies, and how Rouse and Pepper were going to handle the investigation of me taking one hired motor vehicle without me being responsible for the trouble caused.

"Pepper, Rouse, and I walked away from the area to the frontage. Slouch never joined us then. I was led to believe that they had someone in mind, even though within my mind, I thought that Borer oversaw that we were interfering with the main operation, like an organisation behind the big ideal, and wanted to suffocate us under a banner of troublesome diversion."

PEPPER

This operation is operating across the country making millions of bucks. We want to nail those shots!

ROUSE

Could we call on your cooperation, Mr. Willows?

BRANDON

You may have to go through Borer, my boss. Don't touch Whitehall yet. I suspect something is going on right now.

PEPPER

Who's he?

"Pepper said it in a way like he doubt that Borer could handle the assignment; he was pretending to do so even though he believed himself to be one of the tops in the force. At that time, he suggested that and named two chaps he referred to and called Burt and Whitehall who would replace Borer just in case of scenarios in which his department falls on another shoulder."

PEPPER

One of them bright sparks. Think he'll be replacing Borer. They never come this far north, but we would like to nail them before they get to the second and third one.

BRANDON

Okay. Since right now, I plead my innocence before you two, I'll return to my main business of looking after Shank and Borer, seeing that none of them lay any trouble on me about this small imagery. Everybody in business will have to be warned about the son of a bitch—those people who have their accounts there with Mr. Slouch. They normally get about three to four vehicles from each vendor. Course, we always pay by cheque. Anybody can cream off the cheque number and handed to some unscrupulous vendor to change it for them. Could call up the bank and change the account number, if that would help. It's your business anyway.

"Pepper beckoned Slouch to come over and join us."

ROUSE

Could check that out for you. Always traded this way over the telephone?

SLOUCH

Sometimes, we don't even saw our customer or knew who they are. They just order what vehicle they wanted. Sometimes, we have contractors hired to drive our cars to their destination. All the person or firm does is sign the delivery documents and pay as normal or whatever. That vehicle will be writing off and will be back on the road within days of it being sold.

HALF-BALD MAN

Honestly, it would be hard to stop the way we traded now without distressing our customers.

"I supposed Colet could not hear what we were saying over her monitor, so she had crept back to the service counter. The four men sat at one of the table, speaking slowly and low as though anything heard outside an inch would set the place a blaze."

PEPPER

Know of anybody, anybody that would want to screw you, Mr. Willows?

BRANDON

No one immediately coming to mind. But that Malatya bastard may want to. Could name a dozen without thinking. But I don't think they'll go that low. Could be from my past as much. Revenge for my past.

PEPPER

Been up for, you know?

"I assumed that being an undercover cop, he had to bring out my past in front of strangers. If Slouch picked upon it, he may understand the colloquial expression been up for. I then commenced to resent the big-eyed bastard because I had no way of knowing what he was thinking when he was trying to hang me out to dry."

BRANDON

Had nothing to do with what's going on here. You're the employed cops that can't deal with the small timers. So don't you come picking your arseholes around me.

PEPPER

No harm in asking. Burt I'll come to see you shortly.

BRANDON

Pooh! There you had a White guy running around with WPIA cards claiming to be me. No Black guy's going to do that and get away with it, you awful son of a bitch. Let me explain. From the time a Black man enters through the door of White hotel, he becomes a victim of uncalled-for attention. This hotel missed the point.

ROUSE

Hmm...Hmmm. We won't be able to solve the problems without coming together to find out the connection. We're going to do some thorough account exchange right now and exhaust it once and for all.

SLOUCH

Course, we have several depots around the country.

PEPPER

You take all the bookings from here?

SLOUCH

We do.

BRANDON

So, from here, we may be able to check the son of a bitch, and that's my pitch.

PEPPER

Think Borer will want to hear of this?

SLOUCH

Borer deals with drugs and related case now.

BRANDON

No, he deals with surveillance now. Remember him dealing with frauds and related cases not so long ago? I think Whitehall will fall into that slot now. Good experience to have on board—Borer, I mean.

SLOUCH

Hmm...hmm. Well, gentlemen, I think and hope you will do something about this mess. I am counting on it to happen quickly.

ROUSE

Hmm...hmm.... About how much vehicles you lost like this and losing with in this assistance?

"Slouch yelped, got up from the table, and was ready to go back to work. In my mind, I presumed that the unknown person or persons might have had many more of my business card or may mint some other kind that included WA as their benefactor and repeated the game they play again. Again, though they developed convincing attitudes, somebody in the hotel where they pretended to be me must, by now, recollect his/her features."

BRANDON

Not more than four. That's how the trend seems to be moving. If we didn't have a little bit of cash to move around, that son of a bitch would stop our operation in its tract.

SHANK

The force will pay for all this, will it not?

ROUSE

We'll see you get covered, Mr. Slouch.

BRANDON

Fine with me. If that's the case, I'll go along with it. Never dealt with these things before, so it is all new to me.

PEPPER
We'll come back to see you again, Mr. Slouch, to straighten out some edges.

BRANDON
Good.

"Slouch went back to work.

"I had been eyeing Colet. She had frequently been going and coming back to the counter between phone calls. Slouch was with too older White men in his office. Colet, she needed a bronze man to match her colour.

"We had agreed to meet urgently with Borer to have his consent for me to continue with the WAA investigation and, at the same time, helping to apprehend a White man who was going around with my card and bank account number in his pocket, pretending to be me.

"I didn't want to say bye to Colet; I just wanted to check her out. Pepper and Rouse slowly walked unconcerned toward the entrance. I was doing the same when Colet called."

Chapter Twenty-Eight

COLET
   Mr. Willows."

BRANDON
   Oh!

"I walked back toward her. She was leaning sideways on the service counter."

COLET
   Going without saying goodbye? Course, I been looking in your cup to see what you have up your sleeve.

BRANDON
   Didn't you see anything down the trousers?

COLET
   Didn't go that far, just along the chest and up the brain.

BRANDON (*being romantic*)
   Pooh! What did you want to scan, babe?

COLET
   Just what you're thinking.

BRANDON
   Know I wouldn't do that. Have lunch with me one day?

"I knew I was lying; it was a trap."

COLET
When?

BRANDON
Got a number I could call?

COLET
Yeah, I'll write it for you?

BRANDON
Sure. Knows what Jack becomes without a little play?

COLET
Here you are.

"She wrote her number on a sheet of the WA company's writing pads and gave it to me. Then we went on our way home."

The following day...

BORER
Where are you now, Brandon?

BRANDON
Call you 'morrow.

"I folded the sheet in four quarters, stuck it in the breast pocket of my jacket, and slid away. I had hit the evening rush hour at about a third of the journey coming back into the city and didn't encounter any heavy traffic. But then, after the city, I was going NNW. There, I was a delayed a little. But by then, the place where I had passed by the guy trying to fly off the building was clear. Anyway, it was getting late as I remembered that I was driving Shank's car.

"Shank had a couple of months to go before the baby comes and didn't want to drive herself. So she was waiting impatiently for me to get back to take her home. We didn't plan what had hit us that day. I didn't plan about the hotel resort calling WPIA and the vehicle-hiring place, and I didn't plan to meet Colet. Each problem came with its own problem-solving tools.

"Shank wasn't feeling well when we got home, and I had to burn at the stove. I had some stretch rice and a tin of corned beef. It was mixed with broad beans mash, ready-made potatoes, and dark-burned scallion to give it some taste.

"A little over the night, I had a red wine bottle, although Shank did not want to indulge. I downed the glass and a half of the lot. Shank just wanted to have pineapple juice and more pineapple juice like we were part of the Del

Montel family. I guessed that was what the little fellow in her wanted to drink; it was to too early for me to take him to the public house to have his first soda."

BRANDON
I'm sure I could have a quick meal from Mussolini's if I was alone.

SHANK
One minute in women's life they can't cook, and there's trouble.

"She said it as if she meant she was sorry."

BRANDON
Look, doll. You don't understand what I really meant. Only can cook beans and toast bread. Just hope when he grows up he'll know what he has done to you.

"She rested her hand on her paunch and laughed. I was sorry, too; the child was kicking her guts out."

BRANDON
I sure will. No doubt you're going to tell him about the starvation you underwent.

"I decided not to venture out that evening, but I gave Borer a telephone call after I got a wash. I enlightened him with what was going on. However, by then, Pepper had made contact, and he was already aware.
"Fritz had been out on surveillance; BAID was paying him directly for his contract work. Borer had decided I was to help the CID and, while I was doing that, find if there is any drug-related incident that he could lock on as well."

BRANDON
That Pepper guy?

BORER
Know him some time ago, I supposed.

"I was hoping that Borer would let go of any old grudge."

BRANDON
Ask about you and even said he probably....

BORER
I'll get you on his team.

BRANDON
That son of a bitch. I'm going to do it myself! Well, I'll be darned.

BORER
How's Shank?

"Shank was sitting across on one of them stiff chairs for an expectant mother. She had been turned from a beautifully-shaped woman to one in pain and feeling uncomfortable. Her face was dragged; I couldn't believe it, reflecting on my mother carrying me around while my father may have been screwing some other woman to satisfy his immediate necessity."

BRANDON
She's okay beside her general problems. Swollen feet and all that stuff.

BORER
Willows? How're you and Shank getting on? Seeing another woman, aren't you?

"I couldn't see the man, but the feeling I had gotten was the man on the other end knew something and was asking me."

BRANDON
Why the concern?

BORER
Colet is one of us. So my advice is: Don't fool around. Can't tell you what to do; you are your own man. But I will have to hint Shank about it.

BRANDON
Okay. What about Fritz and Mow?

BORER
None of them related to me. But you see, it was the same time when my wife was expecting that I went out, and then Shank came along. Many women, when pregnant, don't like to have sex, and we men like to have it all the while, so we seek any opportunity that presents itself. Worst time to become a womaniser.

BRANDON
Was it Pepper or Rouse? Well, if you had done that, I wouldn't have had her now, boss man.

BORER

Both. Got to keep it clean, Willows. Got to keep ourselves as clean as possible. Cops oing through a bad patch right now, and everybody's looking in our cupboard.

BRANDON

Okay. Thank you for that advice, DIB. Appreciate it.

"I put the phone back onto its hook and went to sit by Shank. I tried to caress her, rubbing her shoulder and working my hands upward to her tender jaw and over to her lips. Then I moved my hand across into her hair and dwelt there for a moment. We were like strangers who had seen each other to make our first love. I knew that the son of a bitch was still kicking his mother's heart out after, but it was worth it to dose the bugger; I got my way."

BRANDON

Everything's okay? Just another piece of advice from your adopted old cop.

SHANK

Did he talk 'bout what you've just did?

BRANDON

No, darling, just a piece of fatherly advice from a White man. He hopes you'll have a good night rest tonight.

"Shank and I settled down after tea to watch TV. I bought a Harden bedding where she could lie down or sit up when she felt like doing so. We had been living on top of our practice for going nine months. On the upper floor, one of the rooms was larger out of the two. That was our living room, decorated in Maria colour and matched for the eye of a woman.

"From the windows, you could see the post office towers and even the or-thunder, a Birmingham City landmark. There was wide open view from there, and in summer, the view was quite pleasant. From the episode of the day, tiredness had run in my body.

"I just reached the train station with my suitcase to catch the train to visit Steve; he was still in the pen. Fritz came from the opposite platform and boarded the train. He was in authority because hag he got on the train before it had driven off. I was running behind, yelling."

BRANDON

That is the train I want! That's the train I want!

"Then my suitcase opened, and all the papers flew out. I stopped to retrieve the papers, but the train was gone.

"It was on the morning when Shank had been giggling like her natural self. I knew that having sex was flirty and shouldn't be carried over the next day unless she wanted more and for me to dose the little bugger again to keep him quiet."

SHANK
Who were you cursing and swearing?

BRANDON
When was that?

SHANK
I thought you were talking about the show, then you started shout. What is going on?

BRANDON
I wasn't.

SHANK
You sure were. Telling the person to stop the train.

BRANDON
Must be Fritz. He wouldn't stop the train to wait for me. Then I had my suitcase, which flew open while I was running to catch the train. I stopped to gather up the papers, and by then, the train was gone.

SHANK
I see. Fritz again, eh? Give the guy a break, man.

BRANDON
You've given him a full hundred percent. I would hold back, say, five for manoeuvre tolerance, just for probability. Can't say why now, but you should. Nothing's hundred percent pure.

"There were scurrying following the car hiring investigation. Borer had asked me to concentrate on the BAID case. However, the following day, DuPont rang and said that he would like to see me at his office to update me on Steve's case. I had seen Mrs. Boot on the same morning. She was in civilian outfit and waved to me.

"I waved back, hoping I would have a word. I went and parked the car, but when I came back onto Soho, she had gone. I went around a couple of corners and peeped into a few of the shops and stores, but I didn't find her.

"Shank got a letter from Savaggy, thanking us for attending his party. She didn't give me the letter to read, but I more or less gathered it contained women stuff and probably with a few lines of gossip from Mrs. Savaggy. Shank was adequately covering the four pages with a little giggle here and there when I left out to go and see DuPont.

"I then gathered that had Mrs. Savaggy been adept with computers or any word processing equipment, she would word process the pages. This, I would let Shank aware of, if she hadn't already guessed and told her to suggest to Mrs. Savaggy, as part of her wasting valuable time to go on part-time course and study modern word processing.

"If she didn't, then it would be no skin off our nose. They could afford what they chose to do on God's land. We were just third party to her husband's chairmanship and his reporting of a saboteur ring going on with his firm. Maybe, just maybe, he wasn't one of the boys from Cambridge or Harrow, Oxford or the sort.

"I was still on my way to see DuPont. Travelling SSE, struggling to come up with what a mess everything had seemed to be. Now, I had wants and needs and wants and needs. Borer wanted to see me at two thirty that afternoon, and I was already running late to see DuPont. I wanted to ring Colet. I wanted to know who the son of a bitch carrying around my account number and business card was.

"What Fritz and Mow had been up to, I did not care; I wanted to be with Shank. There were also other things I needed to know: why Massey wanted to put Steve in the pen and keep him there, who blew Fritz's place, what happened to Tabasco Wall, where's my freedom, who's my friend, what Jupt was doing down in the West Indies, and how Rouse and Pepper were going to handle the investigation.

"Pepper, Rouse, and I walked away from the area to the frontage. Slouch never joined us then. I was led to believe they had someone in mind, an operation like an organisation behind the big deal."

PEPPER
This operation is being conducted across the country, making millions of bucks. We want to nail those shits as well as the insider.

ROUSE
Could we call on your cooperation, Mr. Willows?

BRANDON
You may have to go through Borer, my boss. Don't touch Whitehall yet.

ROUSE
Who's he?

PEPPER
One of them bright sparks. Thinks he'll be replacing Borer. They never come this far north, but we would like to nail them before they get to the third one.

ROUSE

Everybody in business will have to be warned—people who have their accounts here with Mr. Slouch. They normally get about three to four vehicles from each vendor.

BRANDON

Course, we always pay by cheque. Anybody can cream off the cheque number and hand it to some unscrupulous vendor. Could call up the bank and change the account number, if that would help.

Chapter Twenty-Nine

"Pepper beckoned Slouch to come over and join us. I then turned my head toward Pepper, thinking he might say that Burke would be replacing Borer shortly, or he would say how longer Borer's time around would be; he was our leaning stick. However, he wouldn't budge and give the information."

ROUSE

You always traded this way over the telephone?

SLOUCH

Sometimes, we don't even saw our customer or knew who they are. They just order what vehicle they wanted. Sometimes, we have contractors hired to drive our cars to their destination. The firm makes electronic checks on that person or firm and gets them just to sign the delivery document and then left them with the vehicle until they brought it back to us. Then there are some checks ran over to make it ready for the next customer.

SLOUCH

That vehicle will be writing off and will be back on the road within days of it being sold.

HALF-BALD MAN

Honestly, it would be hard to stop the way we traded now without distressing our customers.

"I supposed Colet could not hear what we were saying over her monitor, so she had crept back to the service counter. The four men sat at one of the table, speaking slowly including myself and lowly as though anything heard outside an inch would set the place ablaze."

SMALL HEAD
Know of anybody, anybody that would want to screw you, Mr. Willows?

BRANDON
No one immediately coming to mind. But that Malatya bastard may want to. Could name a dozen without much thinking, but I don't think they'll go that low. Could be from your gang as much—revenge for my past.

PEPPER
Been up for, you know.

"I assumed that being an undercover cop, he had to bring out my past in front of strangers. If Slouch picked upon it, he might understand the colloquial expression 'been up for.' I then commenced to resent the big-eyed bastard but had no way of knowing what he was thinking when he was trying to hang me out to dry."

BRANDON
Had nothing to do with what's going on here. You're the employed cops that can't deal with the small timers. So don't you come picking your arseholes around me.

PEPPER
No harm in asking.

BRANDON
Pooh! There you had a guy running around with WPIA cards, claiming to be me. No Black guy's going to do that and get away with it. That awful son of a bitch. Let me explain.

ROUSE
Hmm...hmm.... We won't be able to solve the problems without coming together to find out the connection. We're going do some account exchange.

SLOUCH
Course, we have several depots.

PEPPER
You take all the bookings from here?

SLOUCH
We do.

PEPPER
    So, from here, we may be able to check the son of a bitch.

BRANDON
    That's my pitch.

PEPPER
    Think Borer will want to hear of this?

BRANDON
    Borer deals with drugs and related cases now and some surveillance that will keep him going after retirement; he'll still have his hand in the operation.

PEPPER
    Remember him dealing in frauds and related cases not so long ago?

BRANDON
    I think Whitehall will fall into that slot now.

ROUSE
    Good experience to have on board—Borer, I mean.

SLOUCH
    Hmm.... Well, gentlemen, I think and hope that you will do something about this mess—counting on it to happen quickly.

BRANDON
    Hmm.... About how much vehicles will we be losing with this assistance in a year?

SLOUCH
    Not more than four. That's how the trend seems to move.

    "Slouch yelped, got up from the table, and was ready to go back to work."

SLOUCH
    The force will pay for all this, will they?

PEPPER
    We'll see you get covered, Mr. Slouch.

BRANDON
    Fine with me. If that's the case, I'll go along with it. Never dealt with these things before, so it is all new to me—another unit under my belt.

PEPPER
　　We'll come back to see you again, Mr. Slouch, to straighten out some edges.

BRANDON
　　Good.

　　"Slouch got up and went back to his work.

　　"I had been eyeing Colet. She had been frequently going and coming back to the counter between phone calls. Slouch was too old of a White man for her. She needed a bronze man to match her colour.

　　"We had agreed to meet urgently with Borer to get his consent for me to continue with the WAA investigation while helping to apprehend a White man who was going around with my card and bank account number in his pocket.

　　"I didn't want to say bye to Colet; I just wanted to check her out. Pepper and Rouse slowly walked toward the entrance, unconcerned. I was doing the same when Colet called."

COLET
　　Mr. Willows.

BRANDON
　　Oh!

　　"I walked back toward her. She was leaning sideways on the service counter."

COLET
　　Going without saying goodbye? Course, I been looking in your cup to see what you have up your sleeve.

BRANDON
　　Didn't you see anything down the trousers?

SHANK
　　I hope she didn't go that far, just along the chest and up the brain.

BRANDON
　　Pooh! Meant that. What did you want to scan, babe?

SHANK
　　Just what are you thinking, Brandon Willows?

BRANDON
What are you up to, Shank? You know I wouldn't do that.

"I know I was lying; it was a trap."

BRANDON
Have lunch with me one day?

SHANK
When is that?

BRANDON
Got a number I could call?

SHANK
Yeah. I'll write it for you?

BRANDON
Sure.

SHANK
Here you are.

"She wrote her number on a sheet of the company's writing pads and handed it to me. Then I went my way."

BRANDON
Call you 'morrow.

"I folded the sheet in four quarters, stuck it in the breast pocket of my jacket, and slid away. I had hit the evening rush hour at about a third of the journey coming back into the city and didn't encounter any heavy traffic. But then, after the city, I was going NSW. There, I was a delayed a little. But by then, the place where the guy trying to fly off the building I had passed by earlier was clear. Anyway, it was getting late as I remembered that I was driving Shank's car.

"Shank had a couple of months to go before the baby comes and didn't want to drive herself. So, she was waiting impatiently for me to get back to take her home. We didn't plan what had hit us that day. I didn't plan about the hotel resort calling WPIA and the vehicle-hiring place, and I didn't plan to meet Colet. Nonetheless, each problem came with its own units of problem-solving tools.

"Shank wasn't feeling well when we got home, and I had to start the stove. I had some stretch rice and a tin of corned beef. It was mixed with mashed broad beans, ready-made potatoes, and dark-burned scallion to give it some taste. A little over the night, I had a red wine bottle which Shank did not want to indulge in. So I downed the glass and half of the lot. Shank just wanted to have pineapple juice and more pineapple juice like we were part of the Del Monte family."

BRANDON
I'm sure I could have a quick meal from Mussolini's if I was alone.

SHANK
One minute in women's life they can't cook and there's trouble.

"She said it as if she meant she was sorry."

BRANDON
Look, doll. You don't understand what I really meant. Only can cook beans and toast bread—what we were brought up on. Never do us any harm in the short run; doesn't know about the longer term. Just hope when he grows up, he'll know what he has done to you.

"She rested her hand on her paunch and laughed. I was sorry, too. The child was kicking her guts out, and there was nothing I could have done to calm it down; I couldn't do more than see her wrench with aggravation."

BRANDON
He sure will know. No doubt you're going to tell him about the starvation you underwent.

"I decided not to venture out that evening. However, I gave Borer a telephone call after I got a wash. I enlightened him of what was going on. But by then, Pepper already made contact and he was already aware.
"Fritz had been out on surveillance for the WAA which was paying him directly for his contract work. Borer had decided that I was to help the CID and, while I was doing that, find if theirs was any drug-related incident he could lock on as well."

BORER
That Pepper guy. Knew him some time ago, I supposed.

"I was hoping that Borer would let go of any old grudge he was carrying for Pepper. Since he never seemed familiar with Rouse, I considered it pointless to bring his name forward in the perusing."

BORER
Ask about you and even say he'll probably get you on his team.

BRANDON
That son of a bitch. Well, I'll be darned.

BORER
How's Shank?

"Shank was sitting across on one of them stiff chairs for an expectant mother. She had been turned from a beautifully shaped woman to one in pain and uncomfortable. Her face was dragged; I couldn't believe it, reflecting on my mother carrying me around while my father might have been screwing another woman to satisfy his immediate necessity out of his polygamous satisfaction."

BRANDON
She's okay beside her general problems of swollen feet and all that stuff.

BORER
Willows, how you and Shank getting on?

"I couldn't see the man, but the feeling I had gotten was that the man on the other end knew something and was asking me."

BRANDON
Why is the concern now, Sir?

BORER
Seeing another woman, aren't you? Colet is one of us, so my advice is, "Don't fool around." Can't tell you what to do; you are your own man. But I will have to hint Shank about it.

BRANDON
Okay. What about Fritz and Mow? Spying on my home life now?

BORER
None of them related to me.

BRANDON
Was it Pepper or Rouse who told you?

BORER
Both. We've got to keep it clean, Willows. We've got to keep ourselves as clean as possible. Cops going through a bad patch right now, and the public body are looking in our cupboard.

BRANDON
Okay. Thank you for that advice, DIB. Appreciate it.

"I put the phone back on to its hook and went to sit by Shank. I tried to caress her, rubbing her shoulder and working my hands upward to her tender jaw and over to her lips. Then I moved my hand across her hair and dwelt there for a moment. We were like strangers that had seen each other to make our first love. I knew that the son of a bitch was still kicking his mother's heart out after, but it was worth it to dose the bugger, and I got my way at that moment."

SHANK
Everything's okay?

BRANDON
Just another piece of advice from your adopted old copper.

SHANK
He did say what you've just did.

BRANDON
No, darling. I just got a piece of fatherly advice from a White man. He hopes you'll ave a good night rest tonight.

"Shank and I settled down after tea to watch TV. I bought a Harden bedding where she could lie down or sit up when she felt like doing so.
"We had been living on top of our practice for going nine months. On the upper floor, one of the rooms was larger out of the two. That was our living room, decorated in Maria colour and matched for the eye of a woman. The other room was decorated for a baby; it was so long ago now that I almost forgot who it was for.
"From the windows, you could see the post office towers and even the or-thunder thundering down over the city's landscape. It was a widely open view from there, and in summer, the view was quite pleasant. As I scanned down from the episode of the day while looking from the balcony, I felt tiredness run into my body. My eyes were getting a bit dim, so I went off to bed, hoping that the next day would arrive with a better understanding of the previous.
"I just reached the train station with my suitcase to catch the train to visit Steve; he was still in the pen. Fritz came from the opposite platform and boarded the train. He was in authority because when he got on the train, it had driven off. I was running behind, yelling my guts out."

BRANDON
That is the train I want! That's the train I want!

"Then, my suitcase opened, and all the papers flew out. I stopped to retrieve the papers, and the train was gone.

"It was on the morning when Shank had been giggling like her natural self. I knew that having sex was flirty and shouldn't be carried over the next day unless she wanted more and for me to dose the little bugger again to keep him quiet. However, I couldn't; all my energy had gone during that session."

SHANK

Who were you was cursing and swearing to?

BRANDON

When was that?

SHANK

I thought...I was talking about the show then you started fuming. What's going on?

BRANDON

I wasn't. It was a bad dream again. I wonder what he's getting up to now?

SHANK

You sure you were telling the person to stop the train? Who was it?

BRANDON

I must be talking in my sleep. 'Pose it must be Fritz; he wouldn't stop the train to wait for me. I had my suitcase, and it flew open while I was running to catch the train. I stopped to gather up the papers, and by then, the train was gone—the same dream I had before.

SHANK

I see. Fritz again, eh? Give the guy a break, man.

"Meanwhile, Borer had just came through the office door; he might have heard our conversation."

BORER

Don't know you've given him a full hundred percent. I would hold back, say, five, for manoeuvre tolerance, just for probability. Can't say now why you've given all of that, but you should know why; nothing's hundred percent pure.

"There were scurrying, following the car hiring investigation. Borer asked me to concentrate on the BAID case, but the following day, DuPont rang and said that he would like to see me at his office to update me on Steve's case. I had seen Mrs. Boot on the same morning. She was in civilian outfit and waved to me happily.

"I waved back, hoping I would have a word. I went and parked my car, but when I came back onto Soho, she had gone. I went around a couple of corners and peeped into a few of the shops and stores, but I didn't find her.

"Shank got a letter from Savaggy, thanking us for attending his party. She didn't give me the letter to read, but I more or less gathered that it contained women's stuff and probably a few lines of gossip from Mrs. Savaggy. Shank was adequately covering the four pages with a little giggle here and there when I left to go and see DuPont.

"I then gathered that Mrs. Savaggy was not adept with computers or any word processing equipment or else she would word process the pages. This, I would let Shank be aware of, if she hadn't already guessed and tell her to suggest to Mrs. Savaggy, as part of her wasting valuable time, to go on part-time course to study modern word processing.

"If she didn't, then it would be no skin off our nose. They could afford what they chose to do on God's land; we were just third party to her husband's chairmanship and his reporting of a saboteur ring going on with his firm. Maybe, just maybe, he wasn't one of the boys from Cambridge or Harrow, Oxford, or the other sort."

Chapter Thirty

"I was still on my way to see DuPont, travelling SSE and struggling to understand what a mess everything came to be. Now, I had wants and needs and wants and needs. Borer wanted to see me at two thirty that afternoon, and I was already running late to see DuPont. I wanted to ring Colet; I wanted to know who the son of a bitch carrying around my account number and business card was.

"I needed to know what Fritz and Mow had been up to, and I wanted to be with Shank. Other things I need to know: 'Why did Massey want to put Steve in the pen and keep him there?' 'Who blew up Fritz's place?' 'What happened to Tabasco Wall?' 'Where's my freedom?' 'Who's my friend?' 'What is Jupt doing down in the West Indies?' and, 'How are Rouse and Pepper going to handle the investigation?'

"Fritz's standard was being a well-known, untrustworthy, and underhanded butcher. When it boiled down to his pound of steak, he wished everything added to it. Somebody else was always in the wrong but not him. I climbed over Borer and Whitehall's heads and arranged to see Steve at the HMPS, Green. I'd been schooled there, and everybody I knew while I was there was still around.

"It was ten or twenty years ago; hence those same pos. Will was still alive and working there; he remembered me as an inmate. Any covert vocabulary would shine on the face like the moon and would be soon picked up by blokes. They went beyond the eyeballs when staring at you and any finite bits of deception would get buried in the skull. Then they would magnetically pluck both eyeballs out. Then they would place them on the table and ask you to take a look.

"I remember, when I was educated there, I walked up to the prison reception. Two guards were standing abreast the entrances. That's being part of my education accentuated when it came to the prison. Schooling there enabled me to understand the environment. It was home to me in straight five years, and a little more if I got caught."

BRANDON

Come to take some statement from Steve Boot—urgent. I represent his co-partner; I just want to collect a few points from him. Can I see him immediately?

PO (POLICE OFFICER)

Who are you then? Going straight now, I see?

"I'd known how to avoid the look he gave me, so I twitched the licence on him."

BRANDON

Steve Boot's lawyer. Can't hang a man going straight now, can you?

PO

Heard you're a private boy now; passed the law business. You became even more bent like all of them?

BRANDON

That's how you come to have a job, and good to hear the admittance that I was helping to keep you blokes employed for sometime here and there. Glad to hear it from the cow's mouth. See? You're still trigger-happy on the gossip stinger.

STEVE'S FRIEND

Doing any good?

BRANDON

Paying the taxpayer to harass me more like paying sweaty armhole like you to stand there and ask silly questions.

PO

You'll be back here soon.

Later...

BRANDON

I reckon that Steve knows about many other things that he was not willing to admit.

"Partial break came when I decided to lean on Steve who was on remand for a few months; he was without any judiciary decision to be prisoned or not. I knew from the earlier discussion that he had some information, but I didn't want to dig too deeper then and at the present time."

STEVE

I don't have anything to say to you. When I help you and you're gone with your big job and then left me here to rot. I did tell you dot, mess about with dem and dem will see you hang first. Dem want to move the factory from where it is now, you know that?

BRANDON

No, I didn't know they were planning to move.

STEVE

Dem employed too many Black people in that spot as well, so dem a move it out to sum other place. Maybe is where dem will employ more of affluent white people.

BRANDON

Think so?

STEVE

I know so. No factories now moves into the Black area and dem that in there dem close dem down almost instantly. Su it ended with Blacks without work or employment, more a dem though.

BRANDON

Political?

STEVE

And social and economic injustice woes. Well, bud, if that's the way they feels, dem a going to do it.

BRANDON

I'm closer to you, man. So look, brother. Help me out, and I'll see what I can do. You heard that I'm a good man. You must' also heard that I have some schooling here, too, and as tough as you old pumper as well; I can pass on some good information from here—in and out a here. So what's it going to be, Steve?

STEVE

Den a way you a say-den, Mr. Willows. Me never know dot, you cum a dis yaw place too?

"He looked at me shrewdly and smiled."

BRANDON
Yes, I was a student here—five years and a little. And if you're not learning anything being in here at all, you'll need your head examined or screwed off and replaced with a new one.

"I remarked that I might have to join by choice the higher learning again for info."

STEVE
That would be something, Mr. Willows. Welcome me; we talk nu. And I'll get information from Bulldozer and I'll lift it for you to hang dem all.

BRANDON
Yes, that's what I'm here for, Steve.

"Borer hinted that the WAA people were talking about the news report, saying they would shortly consider a merger with another major airplane maker bidding to join the new aircraft's development; anyone with information must send it along. I had written to the office and asked to be self-represented at the hearing. I then asked DuPont to strengthen my case with a sort of tie-up a few legal fluffs that may spuriously come away from the garment to stop the evidence I had obtained.

"Shortly after, I went at the PD to see Borer, knowing he might have something himself to say. However, I didn't get anything; he thought we were tailing off the investigation to his liking—only to his liking and not to what he really wanted us to do. He gives us a sword with the two cutting edges alright, but they were dulled out. None of the edges could draw blood should we entered into combat with any of our opponent."

BRANDON
I picked up some vibes—vibes which told me that WAA wants to move the firm from its present location to another location and out of the poorer area; it seems that they wanted a place where they can employ more Whites and less ethnic representation.

BORER
That isn't true.

BRANDON
Yes, it is. Now, I can see the desperation in it for us Blacks. Get a Black guy to write these reports and shove it before the media, telling them it was written by a Black man who sees the move as inevitable as though he's aside with the okay fingers up.

BORER

So tell me, Willows, what have you been up to lately? Know that you visit Steve.

BRANDON

I visited him only as an acquaintance. Can't leave the guy there to rot because neither his wife nor his mother won't go to see him.

BORER

I think I did warn you to keep away from Steve?

BRANDON

Course, you did...but we got inbuilt in all of us a little guardian called "conscience." You know about that, don't you?

"He raised his hand and rested them on the table; he showed his annoyance with me. I assumed he would, but then, Borer asked me to put my card on the table where he rested his hand."

BORER

You're new to this field, Willows, and Shank. Consider your child, first and foremost. Better to have a little jam on your toast than none at all.

BRANDON

Why is it that I smell a treat in your narrations, DIB? I will be requesting a favour from you shortly, Sir. This is to clarify what I now understand. If the company was considering moving to some other place, the agenda behind it is different from the original saboteur stuff talked about at first; somebody trying to sell secrets of the aircraft to Al-Qaeda was a fault.

BORER

What's the purpose of that?

BRANDON

If this was a related incident that I could not comprehend, I have a right to be wary of their plan to move and itchy of their reason. If they applied for grants and were turned down, they might conjure another plot to get the grants so they could move the firm, not for improvement but because the climate demanded for it.

Chapter Thirty-One

BORER

This is one of the big employers in the boroughs. If they move out, our officer will have their jobs cut out for them. Not that we would relish that sort of thing you know.

BRANDON

Yes, Sir. Just getting up and moving out will cause a stench, so they got to rig something up to qualify for the move. Think it's rigged up to get government approval? What about the espionage they reported? Something might be going on. But if things were happening at this moment, it would not be the first time, only that things are now pressing to blow. They want a report from a Black investigator, and this will give them a tune to sing. Who could fit that bill more?

BORER

Okay, when you're ready. Always happy to oblige, son.

"His voice drooped into a drably growl."

BORER

Hmm...while you're not going to take advantage or something outside the law, keep the nastiness out of it if you can, Willows.

BRANDON

I can't work anymore in the mire that I'm already in, DIB. Everybody expects to smell with a bit of perfume when working in that area where shits are; it's the same with those acquainted with the sewer, just shaggier.

"I left the PD that afternoon and went home to seek Shank's advice. Fritz left a message on the answering machine, telling me to meet him at the Dragon

ASAP. The dragon was where we have had our first youthful hard shots of whisky, and we never forgot to stop there when something newsy was in the offing. We moved up rank since, but now, our liquor was reduced to lemonade, water, or orange soda and zilch for the road.

"When I got there, Fritz was in sombre moods; I know what I had to expect. Sometimes, I had wondered if we weren't twins on the opposite diametric; although we had our differences, we can't just do without the other's company, even after years of being apart with the sadness of knowing we weren't on speaking terms because he stole one of my gals."

FRITZ

Savaggy held another party last weekend.

"He twisted the glaze, its clear water twirling around, and looking on. He behaved as though he was a reader of the future."

BRANDON

What are they celebrating this time? Know who were there?

"He popped out of his inner coat pocket a list of names that he handed over for me to look at."

FRITZ

Some of these names were familiar in the circles. What you say, Bran, 'bout Mow and I, you know?

BRANDON

Not now, Fritz; you're getting warm taking on the woman from our office. Tell Borer. Know what that means, don't you?

"I was thinking he might have already hived off something or already sold the list as first copy yet was on its second or third pass around."

FRITZ

Should I and Shank, too? Swear, Bran, shan't give you any trouble.

"He had a smile while he pulled at his warty beard."

BRANDON

Trouble that I can see all the way, Fritz—the amount of time you promised that. Know that Henson chick I'd been playing around with?

FRITZ

Mum called me about something of that nature, but I was in a hurry. I could not hear much of what she was saying—something about a child belonging to Willows. She got a child for Aunt, was saying that belongs to Brandon Willows Jr. Is that the name? What you're going to do, old man? Can't report him and can't let him go down. If he's relation, can't kick him out of the family blood. Know what I mean, Bran? Those old gal always turns up with something. Should have used condom, my cousin.

BRANDON

> More dilemma for me and drama. You will promise me that you'll allow me to break it gently to Shank myself?

"Meanwhile, I briefly discussed about Mow and Fritz getting together.

"It was midnight when Shank had woken me to tell me she was glad. I wasn't sure about Fritz's ability; I reserved my judgement for later. The next morning, I had the chance to run up with names and compared it with the list Fritz had obtained on the computer; how he'd come by it didn't matter to me."

Later....

"A few names were familiar and I already knew about. There was one name, however, that commenced to ring bells in my ear. I screened my mind for the name; it was bugging my operational screw with corrosion inhibitor. Since there was no face to it, I had a hunch that I could not drop for a second during the day.

"At the first WAA hearing, the case presented was why the aircraft should not merge with a worldwide consortium and network and remain in BAID's control. It wasn't long after when correspondence from an unknown firm started to arrive on the WPIA's office which, by then, had opened the flood-gates to uncover who we were dealing with and, doubtfully, whether there were some bastards subjecting us to their investigation. Albeit, the ponds were becoming exceptionally muddy."

DUPONT

> Mrs. Willows, we cannot tell you anymore of the WAA's decision or when it will be meeting again, not unless you pull some strings from the top. Doubtful if this is possible or is the case.

SHANK

> Why are you doing this to us? Trouble on line one.

DUPONT

> Of course, I could send out some papers mistakenly marked "Top secret." No trouble if it comes to your address and your read it and sends it on its way. Savvy?

SHANK

Meaning...like the newspaper? Okay, but we don't want the people to come nosing around at the moment. Okay, we'll see what's in that dispatch.

"Meanwhile, angle on the suspected insider playing gulf at his local club: Massey was with another character who played with him and who had arrived a little earlier. He was well-known to Savaggy. Maybe coincidental, he was playing and mulling in with shattered laughter. Fritz was taking the picture of his companion, Mow. It was during the late summer evening and near the golf course.

"I was at home in the afternoon two weeks later. Fritz and Mow came along to visit dressed up like they were going to the moon. I had asked Fritz to get some shots in his security role. He'd popped out some photographs with shots capturing Mow and another face in the background. It was particularly interesting; that was the face I had the name for."

FRITZ

Careful! Looking as though you're about to fall in love with the picture, Bran.

BRANDON

Who's the face in the background?

FRITZ

Scattered shot—never meant for it to show up; we can't tell how the camera pulls it in so close. Why? Somebody you know?

"I didn't answer; I contacted Borer at once."

BRANDON

I've got a name and a picture. I'll fax you the picture.

BORER

No, don't do that; meet me and bring Mow along if you can get a hold of her. Clever surveillance paying off now—enabled redirection of these sorts of things.

"Shank had shown that she wanted to come along as a mush. I agreed because Mow was with my cousin Fritz that I could not divulge at the emergency meeting. When we got at the PD that afternoon, I stopped off on the ninth floor to see how Pepper and Rouse were getting on. I had just wanted to see if their cannon turned on towards any of the Willows, including me."

PEPPER
It was a matter of fact.

"He was sticking out his guts, being pleased."

PEPPER
We got something on your bloke, just watching him to see who he's making contact with, linking him with the countrywide programme.

BORER
My blokes are good. What you mean? My blokes couldn't do the job?

"Fritz came in the afternoon and I told him what my meeting with Borer was about."

Later....

FRITZ
Whoa! Take it easy? Flying off your pedestal, aren't you, Bran?

BRANDON
Okay, okay. Didn't mean to be mean. I got to be careful about you blokes—trying to pin things on us, that's all.

"Fritz and Mow were not at the WAA hearing a month later, either. Shank went to her normal monthly check-ups after the meeting, and I went with her. I could smell a man and woman as they walked toward us; we were sitting in a waiting department of the clinic."

WOMAN
Mrs. Willows?

SHANK
Why? Yes, I am Mrs. Willows.

POLICE
We are here to arrest you for not attending your court hearing.

BRANDON
When was that? I...I thought that was finished. I was promised that we wouldn't be summoned over the misinterpretation.

"I moved across to the man standing as though on frightened ground, or maybe it was the other way round, like God's earth was his alone. Borer came along with us, as our child was his illegitimate grandson. We knew it was a son because we wanted to know earlier what gender our child had. We asked jokingly whether he could be educated while in the womb to spare the fees and all that."

BRANDON
This is a pregnant woman you're starting to harass.

POLICE
Sorry, Sir. We have to take her in.

BORER
Can't arrest her, not yet, anyway.

POLICE
Got a job to do, Gov. We'll wait until the doctor attends to her. By then, you'll have time to arrange something for her to be home tonight. I know how you feel, Sir, got a little boy myself.

"The old crooking lizards were plausibly contented."

POLICE
Nothing much to do, but she will have to apologize to the court in earnest, Sir.

"I could not hear what Shank and the woman bailiff were saying, but even if it was not evident, the woman was trying her damn best to get us into trouble. We must be at the hand of some men or those blaming the damn taxpayers."

BRANDON
How about if you leave her with me and we'll come along in the morning to make her apologize to the court? Know a couple of bailiffs who'd grant that?

"Shank was feeling some pain but still managed to grin like a talking cat. She was clearly not herself when she expected being arrested with our child a short while ago. How long she would be there would be anybody's guess. Maybe, just maybe, it had commenced to educate from womb; we could count on a barrister of some sort hovering over his mother's case at that time.

"Me, Brandon Willows, and my wife, Shank, set up a detective agency to investigate those who dump waste in waterways, but one day, my father-in-law who was a police detective sergeant and also Shank's illegitimate father, offered us a lucrative investigating job. That job would probably set us up for life, but it was too big and, when considered, could wipe us out if it went wrong.

"Meanwhile, I just came home from prison and was approached by another prisoner wanting me to conduct an investigation for him; his wife seemed to be hooked up with some guy while he was in prison. He got bags of cash to spend for us, but Borer, Shank's unclaimed father, told us to refuse the job and go with his offer instead.

"We took both jobs but kept the cash baron out of Borer way, keeping it unknown to him until things commenced to form a bigger and far more corrupted base than we had expected, with cover-ups and lies only to get the company from its present location to an overseas premises or elsewhere."

Chapter Thirty-Two

MAN
> We'll go back to the office, but promise me, Mrs. Willows, that you'll come up to the court in the morning. I'll arrange for you to see a judge quickly.

"He then wrote the time when Shank would attend the court next morning on a bailiff's pad.

"I asked Borer to let me take some statement from Steve as part of the filing system. Steve got into the crowd where carpet layers were as thick as an old barn house design, under cover and over. He was employed at WAA, in low class work, not of his choice but of where the system placed him. Steve was Black, but although he was educated in England, he had seen his White schoolmates excel. Steve was put in charge of shifting papers at the place for filing. He'd noticed the name I'd shown him and recognized that it was a guy named Sawyers.

"In our investigation, we found out that Sawyers had been registered dead for some time. However, the firm was still paying him a wage and his name continued to crop up on the filing system. He was being paid the checks in wage, as though he was alive and well able to function."

STEVE
> Come along there sometime, but not often. Make me see.

"He paused for a minute or so after he took a closer look."

STEVE
> I think...his name crops up a few times, well, around de place when I was filing away some of de documents. He is de hit man for BAID, I hear. He kills people, so you watch yourself and him.

"Meanwhile, a long lens binocular I had planned on WAA was scrambled over the gate from the woodland overlooking the firm's entrance. Later that afternoon, along drove a grey-coloured Jaguar type saloon. It went through the gate and stopped. A character came out of the car, but it was not the driver. He walked up to the door and through the reception."

BRANDON
Could be anybody. But that walk seems familiar.

"I then called Shank's attention; she was going to say something rather shocking, it seemed. She paused and dug the knifepoint into the bread I bought for lunch."

SHANK
Think him shit on you again, Bran?

BRANDON
Suspect Fritz. Isn't that so, doll? Entirely a matter of the guy being some big, selfish dirty bast—

SHANK
Don't swear. I know he's a shit house brick.

BRANDON
Exactly!

SHANK
What? He makes us a few bobs, though.

BRANDON
Your father must've hated what you love, doll—desperate man.

"I then knew that, from the convincing evidence compiled, we weren't able to keep it under wraps any longer. It's a matter of who gets hurt and who would be hurting both of us in depth.

"At the WAA enquiry two days later, the prisoner came in and was pining against two HMPS officers.

"Later that day, just before the hearing, I made my way to a row behind where Borer was seated in the court with his colleagues. Mow was not invited at the hearing, but Fritz was summoned to appear as a key witness. They were late coming in with Steve."

BRANDON
Sure he'll be here in time, DIB?

BORER
 Be patient, Brandon.

"Shortly during the hearing, two persons from HMPS came through the heavy-gauged door. Steve was in the middle, handcuffed to both, but he was our key witness whose given evidence the Crown Court sorted almost at once."

STEVE
 Sawyers have been dead for some time now.

"He pointed to the man on the opposite end."

STEVE
 That is de man I always know as Sawyer, but that one there...

"He pointed at Massy first."

STEVE
 And that one there...

"He pointed at Savaggy."

STEVE
 Bad men's dem. Is real sleaze bag dem is, and that one too with the warty beard...

"He pointed to Fritz."

STEVE
 Dem talking about Al-Qaeda want to take over the company. Lie dem is telling.

BORER
 The old proverb can never be wrong, Willows. "Don't put all your eggs in one basket." That's what it's all about—flushing out the bad men. One down, many more to go, those sons of bitches.

BRANDON
 That's my cue. Yeah, I'll remember that for a long time.

"He leaned across on the shiny courtroom seats and whispered."

SHANK

Just who is your friend? The one who dip his finger in the bowl with you. Isn't that so, Willows?

BRANDON

Not mine. Those two bastards' behaviour can never be controlled. Don't know how my aunt came to bear such a b...!

"I whispered loudly, unconcerned of who would hear me."

BORER

All right, Willows; got your point. It was just an exercise, just in case.

"Another two mouths burden on the taxpayers to feed— nothing big then. I closed the book. Borer was still holding out that I would be one of the good guys. It could certainly work because Shank became his adopted daughter, still oblivious that he really was her father. However, he was not so sure about me.

"When Shank got her baby, she promised to do the matrimonial side a 'things.

"Because it's a buzzing industry for spies and espionages practicing their trade, for the likes of Fritz and his henchmen, maybe they did not have enough revulsion to comprehend when they sold the development to another agent. They did not benefit their insatiable appetite for the higher-up's living.

"They could still play the puppet on the strings. Although removed away from their action zone, or in prison, they could still operate efficiently. Steve's case came up for hearing; he was freed from all charges. What happened to the crow that was following him around? It disappeared. Massey's son, Bulldozer, was released, too, and Shank and I asked both Fritz and Massey's son, Bulldozer, to join WPIA. Maybe, just maybe, we could get something more out of them; it was to be considered.

"With the aircraft's base, they propagated that to move a firm, there had to be big a reason, so they came up with a plan: their plan was to scull the government bluffs, hive off the cash given for the removal, and set up another fuddy-duddy scam somewhere else. However their coverts manipulation was highlighted at the court but then the rendering has been left for WPIA to continue inherently to investigate and reported back to the surveillance team with Borer remain in the driving seat. To be continue.

TABASCO

Petsu Henson's parents did not just move her away from you; she had set her whole gaud damn family against you, including your offspring. As much as you want to, you'll never get to see the child either. I paid their fares and sent them almost to the North Pole—never hear from them again. Spoiling the good reputation.

PEPPER
>Well, plant your seed. Now, it's time for reaping; you've passed your entire test.

BRANDON
>It'll go on for a long time, I suppose, with Shank, me, and our boy.

BORER
>Not for a long time yet.

TABASCO
>Know you're a fighter. Who is Shank, your wife's parents?

BRANDON
>I'm waiting for Shank to have the baby 'cause we have a wedding to attend down the West Indies. Just waiting to hear from Jupt and ask if the date is fixed to marry our Aunty Quam.

BORER
>My grandson must get the right birth in this country, Brandon. Shank will remain with you until such time. Course, if you could oblige me that piece?

Kotch is written in sequels. This is the first of many books planned. The story of all the characters is fictional and bears no resemblance to any individual whether living or dead while the geography remains the same.